CHRISTMAS IN MY HEART

17

JOE L. WHEELER

Pacific Press® Publishing Association
Nampa, Idaho
Oshawa, Ontario, Canada
www.pacificpress.com

Copyright © 2008 by
Joe L. Wheeler in association with Greg Johnson, president, WordServe Literary Group
All rights reserved
Printed in the United States of America

Cover design by Steve Lanto
Cover art by iStockphoto.com
Interior illustrations from the library of Joe L. Wheeler
Inside design by Aaron Troia

Currier & Ives cover illustrations were featured on the first sixteen covers of the Christmast in My Heart® series. Since there exists only a limited number of such horizontal scenes, we have secured additional period winter scenes that will seamlessly mesh with the Currier & Ives ones.

Christmas in My Heart® is a registered trademark of Joe L. Wheeler and may not be used by anyone else in any form. Visit Joe Wheeler's Web site at www.joewheelerbooks.com. Published in association with WordServe Literary Group, 10152 S. Knoll Circle, Highlands Ranch, CO 80130.

Additional copies of this book are available by calling toll-free 1-800-765-6955 or by visiting www.adventistbookcenter.com.

Library of Congress Cataloging-in-Publication Data

Wheeler, Joe L., 1936-   comp.
     Christmas in my heart. Book 17.

     1. Christmas stories, American. I. Title:
Christmas in my heart. Book 17.

ISBN 13: 978-0-8163-2286-2
ISBN 10: 0-8163-2286-4

08 09 10 11 12 • 5 4 3 2 1

Dedication

Where my own stories are concerned, it takes many people to help hammer them into shape. Each of the individuals I have chosen to mercilessly attack my precious word-children brings a uniquely different vantage point, just as was true with the proverbial "Six Blind Men of Hindustan," each approaching the elephant from a different angle or direction.

One of these brutally candid readers, because of his profession as an advertising copywriter, has not only the ability, but also the propensity and inclination to reduce my verbiage down to bare metal. Being used to reducing a message to the fewest possible words, he ruthlessly suggests the same type of word reduction in my stories, even when knowing full well that I will screech at having to part with any of my words, phrases, sentences, and paragraphs. In the end, the synthesis is better than what went before.

Consequently, it gives me great pleasure to dedicate *Christmas in My Heart* 17, our fifty-first story anthology, to our beloved, cherished, and esteemed son,

GREGORY LANCE WHEELER
of
MIAMI, FLORIDA.

Books by Joe L. Wheeler

Abraham Lincoln: A Man of Faith and Courage
Best of Christmas in My Heart I
Candle in the Forest and Other Christmas Stories Children
    Love
Christmas in My Heart, books 1–16
Christmas in My Heart Treasuries (4)
Christmas in My Heart, audio books 1–6
Christmas in My Soul, gift books (3)
Dick, the Babysitting Bear and Other Great Wild
    Animal Stories
Easter in My Heart
Everyday Heroes
Great Stories Remembered, I, II, III
Great Stories Remembered, audio books I–III
Great Stories Remembered Classic Books (12 books)
Heart to Heart Stories of Dads
Heart to Heart Stories of Moms
Heart to Heart Stories of Friendship
Heart to Heart Stories for Grandparents
Heart to Heart Stories of Love
Heart to Heart Stories for Sisters
Heart to Heart Stories of Teachers
Owney, the Post Office Dog and Other Great Dog Stories
Remote Controlled
Smoky, the Ugliest Cat in the World and Other Great Cat
    Stories
St. Nicholas: A Closer Look at Christmas
Soldier Stories
Stories of Angels

Tears of Joy for Mothers
The Twelve Stories of Christmas
Time for a Story
What's So Good About Tough Times?
Wildfire, the Red Stallion and Other Great Horse Stories
Wings of God, The

Acknowledgments

Introduction: "A *St. Nicholas* Christmas," by Joseph Leininger Wheeler. Copyright © 2008. Printed by permission of the author.

"President for One Hour," by Fred P. Fox. Published in *St. Nicholas*, December 1894. Original text owned by Joe L. Wheeler. Fred Fox wrote for popular magazines during the second half of the nineteenth century.

"Kane and Pard," by Addison Howard Gibson. Published in *St. Nicholas*, January 1913. Original text owned by Joe L. Wheeler. Addison Howard Gibson wrote for popular magazines around the turn of the twentieth century.

"In Clean Hay," by Eric P. Kelly. Published in *St. Nicholas*, December 1928. Original text owned by Joe L. Wheeler. Eric Philbrook Kelly (1884–1960) was born in Amesbury, Massachusetts. He spent his academic career teaching English and journalism at Dartmouth College. Author of *The Trumpeter of Krakow* and *The Blacksmith of Vilno*. No other American writer has done more to bring Polish history to life for American readers.

"Where the Christmas Tree Grew," by Mary Eleanor Wilkins Freeman. Published in *St. Nicholas*, January 1888. Original text owned by Joe L. Wheeler. Mary Eleanor Wilkins Freeman (1852–1930) was born in Randolph, Massachusetts. She is best known for stories and novels of frustrated lives in New England villages. Her best-known books are *A Humble Romance and Other Stories*, *A New England Nun and Other Stories*, and *Pembroke*.

"Something for Aunt Jane," by Elizabeth Flint Wade. Published in *St. Nicholas*, January 1911. Original text owned by Joe L. Wheeler. Elizabeth Flint Wade wrote for popular magazines around the turn of the twentieth century.

"Santa Sylvia," by T. Morris Longstreth. Published in *St. Nicholas*, December 1923. Original text owned by Joe L. Wheeler. Thomas Morris Longstreth (1886–1975) was a prolific writer of stories and novels during the first half of the twentieth century. Among his published works are *Tad Lincoln, President's Son*; *Two Rivers Meet in Concord*; and *Henry Thoreau: American Rebel*.

"Baby Deb 'P'ays' for the Christmas Goose," by John Russell Coryell. Published in *St. Nicholas*, January 1885. Original text owned by Joe L. Wheeler. John Russell Coryell (1851–1924) was born in New York City. Originator of the Nick Carter books. Author of such books as *The American Marquis* and *Fighting Against Millions*.

"A Snowbound Christmas," by Frances Cole Burr. Published in *St. Nicholas*, December 1896. Original text owned by Joe L. Wheeler. Frances Cole Burr wrote for popular magazines around the turn of the twentieth century.

"Hetty's Letter," by Katharine Kameron. Published in *St. Nicholas*, January 1883. Original text owned by Joe L. Wheeler. Katharine Kameron wrote for popular magazines during the second half of the nineteenth century.

"A Substitute for Mildred," by Helen M. Girvan. Published in *St. Nicholas*, December 1925. Original text owned by Joe L. Wheeler. Helen Girvan wrote for popular magazines during the first half of the twentieth century.

"A Random Shot," by Marion Hill. Published in *St. Nicholas*, January 1893. Original text owned by Joe L. Wheeler. Marion Hill wrote for popular magazines around the turn of the twentieth century.

"The Cherry-Colored Purse," by Susan Fenimore Cooper. Published in *St. Nicholas*, January 1895. Original text owned by Joe L. Wheeler. Susan Fenimore Cooper (1813–1894) was the daughter of James Fenimore Cooper and was born in Cooperstown, New York. Among her books are *Rural Hours*, *Rhyme and Reason of Country Life*, and *Rural Rambles*.

"Ermee's Christmas Doll," by Alice Josephine Johnson. Published in *St. Nicholas*, December 1899. Original text owned by Joe L. Wheeler. Alice Josephine Johnson wrote for popular magazines around the turn of the twentieth century.

"The Snowbound Santa Claus," by Izola L. Forrester. Published in *St. Nicholas*, December 1905. Original text owned by Joe L. Wheeler. Izola L. Forrester (1878–1944) was born in Pascoag, Rhode Island. She is best known for the Polly Page series of books.

"Where Journeys End," by Beth Bradford Gilchrist. Published in *St. Nicholas*, December 1915 and January 1916. Original text owned by Joe L. Wheeler. Beth Bradford Gilchrist (1879–1958) was born in Peacham, Vermont. Besides being a prolific writer of short stories, she also wrote books such as *The Life of Mary Lyon*, *Trails End*, and the Helen series.

* * * * *

Contents

A St. Nicholas *Magazine Christmas*

Joseph Leininger Wheeler

The *St. Nicholas* Christmas Stories

For this very special *Christmas in My Heart* 17, representing as it does the transition from Review and Herald® to Pacific Press®, I decided to do something very different from anything I'd ever done before: take the sixty-six years of the greatest child/teen magazine of all time and choose the most moving Christmas stories ever to appear in those pages.

Serendipitously, I discovered in the process that not only had I put together one of the most memorable Christmas story anthologies ever to see print, I had—unknowingly—also re-created an age. A very special age . . . a time like no other. A time so different from ours that it desperately needed an introduction like this one, so readers could better understand the characters, settings, and times in which the stories took place.

Also, I felt readers would appreciate a short history of the magazine itself and its impact upon the age.

The Santa Claus variable

Way back at the beginning of this series, in 1992, I made my position on Santa Claus clear: that Christ alone is the reason for the season, not Santa Claus. Having said that, however, I recognize that the Santa Claus persona is interwoven into our Christmas season. Indeed, my conservative minister father donned a Santa Claus suit every Christmas before he handed out our gifts. Consequently, while I've excluded Christmas stories that glorify Santa Claus, I have welcomed stories in which Santa's role is a subsidiary one, one in which he is merely a vehicle for gift giving. Since this is the role of the two Santa characters in the stories included in this collection, I feel comfortable including them.

How the magazine came to be

St. Nicholas began to make itself indispensable in 1873. It held its readers in a rapturous trance for two days a month, and filled their dreams for the other twenty-eight. If you read it as a child, you remember the intensity of anticipation with which you anticipated its coming; the keen disappointment and anxiety if it was late; the tremendous eagerness with which you tore off the wrapper; the little surge of resentment within you if somebody else opened it first. You remember the delight as you turned the pages and gave the pictures and titles the first hasty look; the delectable "feel" of it in your hands. How lovingly you turned every leaf and scanned every page—as you drew near the last pages your heart sank a little, and you tried to assure yourself that "there must be a whole lot more yet!" And every story, every article, every picture, was read and studied until it fairly burned itself into your brain.

—"Fifty Years of St. Nicholas," *St. Nicholas*, November 1923, p. 18.

In human history, there has never been anything like *St. Nicholas* magazine. When it began publication, the terrible Civil War had been over a scant eight years. Louisa May Alcott's *Little Women* had been born six years earlier. It had been only four years since the "golden spike" was driven into a railroad track in Utah, uniting the nation coast to coast for the first time. Stanley had finally tracked down Livingstone in darkest Africa just two years earlier.

The year was 1873. On September 20, Wall Street reeled due to a financial panic—hardly an auspicious time in which to start a magazine for children and teenagers (the first issue appearing at Thanksgiving). But Roswell Smith (1829–1892), legendary publishing tycoon (cofounder of Scribners and founder of the Century Publishing Company), had a dream. He had the money—all he lacked was a visionary editor. He found that in Mary Mapes Dodge (1831–1905), a mother of two sons who was forced by the untimely death of her husband to strike out on her own. Eight years before, she'd been elevated to the pinnacle of popularity in America by the publication of her perennial bestseller, *Hans Brinker, or the Silver Skates*. She proved to be the perfect choice.

Roswell Smith wore big boots. What he envisioned was nothing less than a magazine that would fill a huge vacuum in the English-speaking world—become a child's window into the world; become the one magazine no child in America would wish to grow up without; become a magazine that the world's greatest writers and artists would flock to, each wanting to become a part of it.

Mary Mapes Dodge and her associate editors, Frank Stockton and William Fayal Clarke, pulled it off. A veritable who's who of artists and writers rushed to offer their services: artists such as Arthur Rackham, Maxfield Parrish, Howard Pyle, A. B. Frost, Frederic Remington, Charles Dana Gibson,

Arthur Keller, James Montgomery Flagg, John La Farge, and Reginald Birch; and authors and poets such as Jack London, George Barr McCutcheon, Rudyard Kipling, Anthony Hope, James Barrie, Alfred Lord Tennyson, Joel Chandler Harris, Robert Louis Stevenson, Mark Twain, Mary E. Wilkins, Louisa May Alcott, Henry Wadsworth Longfellow, Bret Harte, Josephine Daskom Bacon, James Russell Lowell, Kate Douglas Wiggin, William Cullen Bryant, John Greenleaf Whittier, William Dean Howells, T. Morris Longstreth, Eugene Field, and Francis Hodgson Burnett.

Faithfully, for two-thirds of a century, over 1,200 pages of fascinating reading material were published each year. During the magazine's first fifty years, there were only two editors: Dodge and Clarke, so the continuity was seamless. *St. Nicholas* was like an answer to prayer for the millions of parents and children. In a very real sense, its pages represented the only real education hundreds of thousands of children and teenagers ever had. And the editors kept the faith. To their credit, they realized that children are the toughest of critics: their decisions quick, accurate, and final. You may occasionally fool them once—but rarely twice.

Not only did *St. Nicholas* provide an encyclopedic introduction to the entire world—history, biography, religion, literature, art, music, mythology, biology, architecture, anthropology, philosophy, technology, folklore, popular culture, etc., it also kept readers abreast of fast-breaking current events. And without preaching or moralizing, the magazines helped inculcate principles of right living in its readers: character traits such as integrity, kindness, self-sacrifice, empathy, industry, courage, fortitude, self-respect, patriotism, respect for their elders, sportsmanship, etc.—traits that bridged to the golden rule and service for others. Interwoven into the very fabric of the magazine was God's leading in each of our lives. Thus, in its sixty-six

years, *St. Nicholas* had a huge impact on an entire people.

Case in point, one never-to-be-forgotten day, Jack London (1876–1916), a San Francisco wharf rat who'd been abandoned by his father, wandered into a public library, picked up a copy of *St. Nicholas*, read it, and resolved to make something of his life. Later, he would write for the magazine himself.

Readers and critics speak out

My children read it. Their children read it. I, the grandfather, hang around to grab it when they lay it down.
–Gustav Kobbé

Following is a small sampling of responses from those who knew the magazine firsthand:

It was the friend and companion of my youth.
—Frank Nelson Doubleday

St. Nicholas *is the best child's periodical in the world.*
—John Greenleaf Whittier

I think that St. Nicholas *made a novelist of me. It was more than an inspiration; it was an incentive.*
—George Barr McCutcheon

There was nothing like St. Nicholas—*it couldn't be done.*
—James Montgomery Flagg

The best of all periodicals ever published for children.
—*New York Tribune*

It was my friend and guide for many years of my boyhood. Bound volumes have been read and re-read by one after another of

our children and our neighbors' children.
—David Grayson [Ray Stannard Baker]

St. Nicholas—*the acknowledged leader of all periodicals for boys and girls not only in America, but in the world.*
—Educational Journal

No other periodical has done more to teach its readers the principles of right living; yet how few of them realize it until they grow up!
—Leroy Fairman

One memory that lingers with me . . . is of the monthly arrival of St. Nicholas. There were three of us boys, and as I was the youngest, my turn was naturally last, and I can recall even now . . . the sense of injustice which this stirred in me. We all read St. Nick through—the serials first, for we were impatient to know what new adventures befell our heroes and (let me confess) heroines; then the stories, the historical sketches, the League, and even the puzzles.
—Henry Steele Commager

The editors kept some of the most memorable letters written to the magazine by their young readers. Among them are these:

My sister has taken you for six months, but—well, I get the mail!

My grandmother gives me St. Nicholas for Christmas every year, and I think I love it better than anyone else I know, though I never saw anybody who didn't think it the best magazine ever printed.

I am always waiting on the front porch the first of the month, waiting for you; and when you come, O Boy! I am dead to the world.

The world *St. Nicholas* readers lived in

So different from ours was the world of 1873–1939 that it seems imperative that we discuss it a little before you burrow into these Christmas stories.

During the first generation of readers (1873–1895), train travel represented the fastest speed known to man. In towns not reached by railroads, transportation was dominated by the horse (pulling a carriage, wagon, or sleigh). Steamboats plied inland waterways, and steamships ruled supreme on the high seas.

The telegraph was the wonder of this generation, for it tied the world together. Not surprisingly, whatever action a given town might provide was, more often than not, found in the telegraph office; the telegraph operator often a star. The superstars that boys yearned to emulate were the railroad engineers on land and the steamship captains on water.

Home life remained rather primitive by today's standards. Relatively few homes had indoor plumbing. Electricity would be slow in reaching rural America (where the majority of people still lived). To most people, the telephone was merely an invention they'd heard about but couldn't imagine using in their homes. The center of home life was the stove, kitchen, or fireplace—here is where family reading took place in the evenings. And they'd gather around the piano to sing. In the summer months, they'd gravitate to the front porch.

Buried as the current generation is in paper, it may be hard for children today to conceptualize how rare paper was back then. So rare, in fact, that children, both at home and at school, tended to write with chalk on slate rather than using a pencil on paper. It is an eye-opening experience to study letters that have survived from that era and see how often they wrote upside down between the lines and on the flip side of the paper as well, rather than resort to finding another sheet of paper. Not until 1884, when Waterman began marketing the first ink-storing pen, was there much of a writing alternative to the goose-quill pen.

Generally speaking, the role of women was unenviable. Few careers were open to them. Girls were trained to become wives and mothers, and once married lost what identity they had, henceforth merely adding "Mrs." to their husbands' names. Thus, when a girl came of age, society expected her to marry and "settle down." Especially in rural America, girls were expected to marry early (usually from fourteen to seventeen years of age) and boys a bit later (fifteen to nineteen). Since there was no reliable birth control, children came on an average of one every two years, hence large families were the norm. No small thanks to the failure of doctors and midwives to wash their hands between patients, untold millions of women died of puerperal fever or childbirth "complications"—hence men tended to go through three wives in a lifetime. If a young woman did not marry, society stigmatized her as a "spinster" and ostracized her. The workload carried by women in those pre-electricity and pre-indoor plumbing days was brutal, making them old before their time.

Medicine was still such a primitive profession that most any disease was likely to terminate a child's life. The result was that contemporaries were almost paranoid about the subjects of disease and death.

The economy was in such a perpetual state of flux that the nation reeled from one financial panic (or depression) after another: 1873, 1893, 1901, 1929 (the worst Depression of all). Because there was no federal protection for bank accounts as we know it today, every time a panic hit, banks failed and depositors lost everything they owned. Since credit cards wouldn't come into regular use until the 1960s and 1970s, one either had money or one didn't—consequently, a penny, nickel, or dime really meant something then. As a result, children were forced to be extremely frugal with what little hard money they were given or earned. With comparatively little money in circulation, especially in rural areas, a barter economy took its place. People had a horror of debt because it had not been long since debtors were often hauled off to prison until those debts were paid. And, when old, there being no Social Security and precious few pensions, all too many of those who'd lost their money and assets and had no children who'd take them in, ended up in that most dreaded place: the poorhouse—at the mercy of those who ran it.

The biggest craze of this generation was the bicycle. Indeed, it was virtually an epidemic during the 1880s and 1890s. Thanks to railroads, time itself had to be regulated; otherwise who would know when to board a train or meet one? Because of this, in 1883 the continent was divided into four time zones, and clocks and watches were hereafter synchronized relative to the prime meridian in Greenwich, England. The result: these timetables dramatically increased people's awareness of time and the pace of living.

During the second *St. Nicholas* generation (1895–1917), the pace of life sped up even more. By the late 1890s, the automobile was coming in and striking terror in the hearts of horses now forced to share roads with them. By 1900, eight thousand automobiles were in use. By 1903, the first motorcar had crossed the continent. It was also in 1903 that Wilbur and Orville Wright, in Kitty Hawk, North Carolina, launched the age of aviation.

Electricity, indoor plumbing, refrigeration, electric

washing machines, etc., began to transform the lives of women, as did advances in medicine. (Finally, women began living into their forties and fifties.) The Bessemer steel I-beam made the construction of skyscrapers possible. In 1913, Henry Ford introduced the concept of the assembly line, thereby revolutionizing industry around the world.

But life remained tough. Even in 1915, one-third of Americans worked up to twelve hours a day, seven days a week, with rarely a vacation day off—all in order to earn thirty dollars a month.

The third *St. Nicholas* generation (1917–1939) began in trauma with the entrance of America into the so-called Great War (World War I). Since most men were in the military, 1,400,000 women entered the workplace. After the war ended, many women were reluctant to climb back into the boxes society had ordained for them.

By 1929, over five million cars had been built, and there were now almost seven hundred thousand miles of paved roads in America. However, October 29 of that year brought the beginning of the most terrible financial crash in American history. Contrary to what many assume, it was not a one-day plunge but rather a gradual decade-long period of decline that never seemed to hit bottom. The Midwest Dust Bowl, a terrible drought in the Great Plains, compounded the national misery. Millions roamed the country in a desperate search for jobs or food. The entire era can be summed up in six plaintive words: *Brother, can you spare a dime?* For in those days, a dime might mean the difference between eating and not eating.

It was during this terrible crucible of anguish that so many American institutions collapsed. Publishing companies and magazines too. Sadly, after holding on for ten long years, even that wondrous magazine, *St. Nicholas*, was forced to close its doors for the last time in 1939.

* * * * *

Now that you better understand the world the characters in these fifteen stories were living in, it is time for us to move on into that storied world.

Enjoy!

CODA

I look forward to hearing from you! Please do keep the stories, responses, and suggestions coming—and not just for Christmas stories. I am putting together collections centered on other genres as well. You may reach me by writing to:

Joe L. Wheeler, PhD
P.O. Box 1246
Conifer, CO 80433

May the Lord bless and guide the ministry of these stories in your home.

* * * * *

Sources used:

Henry Steele Commager, *The St. Nicholas Anthology* (New York: Random House, 1916, 1948), xix–xxi.

"Fifty Years of St. Nicholas," *St. Nicholas*, November 1923, 16–23.

President for One Hour

Fred P. Fox

Fifteen-year-old Tom Martin was the mainstay of his widowed mother. Yet, when the chilling news came over the telegraph wires that a train had broken apart and carnage on the rails was only minutes away, Tom hesitated not a second.

Better that one boy should give up his life than hundreds of lives be lost.

* * * * *

This was the lead story in St. Nicholas' only Christmas treasury: St. Nicholas Christmas Book, in 1920.

* * * * *

It was just eight o'clock as the passenger train pulled out of the Wayville station on the morning of December 24, 1891. The train was heavily laden with jovial people either bound for their eastern homes or festive holiday shoppers going to the city to purchase the last supply of presents that were to make the coming day the happiest of the year.

The mail car and express cars were laden to overflowing with many odd-shaped packages, and even the spaces in the vestibules between the cars had to be utilized for pouches and packages, so great was the jam of Christmas presents.

If it was a jolly crowd that left the little station, it was not an unhappy one that remained. The fog had so settled down upon and around everything that the little lamp in the telegraph and ticket office shed but a feeble light upon the individuals seated around the stove. There is always a crowd in a country station at train time, and in spite of the rules, a few privileged persons always found their way into the office.

Merrily the telegraph instrument ticked away, sending its messages of hope or grief across a continent. As he sat beside the instrument, Fred Clarke, the operator, once in a while shared a bit of electric gossip to the entertained listeners. "Number Thirteen is five minutes late at Bloss," he remarked. Then he smiled as he said, "The general manager has just left High Ridge on his 'special,' coming west. He must have a jolly party with him, for he has ordered fourteen dinners at Glenmore to be ready when he arrives there. His car will pass here at nine ten."

"What engine's pulling the 'special'?" asked Bob Ford, one of the listeners.

"Number Thirty-nine."

"That's Father's old engine," spoke up Tom Martin, a dark-eyed, dark-haired boy of fifteen years, who had been gazing intently into the fire. "He used to run her on all the specials, until he was killed in the accident at Oak Bridge two years ago."

"Right you are, lad," said Bob Ford, "and it's many the time I fired for him on old Thirty-nine. He was as brave and as true a man as ever pulled a lever. You used to ride with us often too—didn't you, Tom?"

"Yes; until one day the general manager saw me sitting in the cab and issued an order that after that day no one but

regular employees in the discharge of their duties should ride upon the engines. I have never been on an engine since; but I learned a great deal about them—didn't I, Bob?"

"Yes, you did, Tom; and, for a boy, you can do as much about an engine as any youngster I know. I would rather have you around than many a fellow I know who's now running an engine. What are you doing now?"

"Since Father's death I do whatever I can to help support my mother, and I find enough to keep me out of mischief. I attend night school, and during the day, I carry the mail between the depot and town, carry dinners and lunches for the men, sell papers, and deliver messages. Besides, I am Fred's pupil and have learned telegraphy."

"Are you making a living at all these odd jobs?"

"Yes, I am. But, of course, I can't make what Father made, and we are trying to pay off the mortgage on the house. I do wish, though, I could do better. Here it is Christmastime, and I have been saving money for six months in order to buy Mother a nice warm cloak, but when I came to price them I found that the five dollars and a half I had saved wouldn't get anything at all like what I wanted. It would take three dollars more, at least. How I would like to have surprised my dear old mother! But then, no matter; I can get her something else that's nice, and we will have a merry Christmas anyway."

"You say you can telegraph," said Bob, after a moment. "What are the wires saying now?"

"The operator at High Ridge is asking whether Number Fourteen left here on time. What's that?" he continued excitedly. "Keep still! Rockville is saying 'Freight train—Number Thirty-three—broke into three sections—at Cantwell. Engineer—thinking there was one break and that rear section was under control—started back to couple on. Dense fog—met middle section coming at full speed—engineer and fireman thrown from engine. Engine and three cars running east downgrade at full speed.' That's terrible!" Fred said. "But listen—'Middle section, one mile behind, just passed—ten loaded stockcars—Jack Flynn clinging to rear car. Must stop train if you can. If Fourteen has not yet left, switch her to westbound track or she'll be lost.' " Then the instrument stopped ticking.

"Is that right, Fred?" Bob asked the operator, as soon as he found his breath, "or has Tom been joking with us?"

"It's all true!" answered Fred. "That's just what's happened! What shall we do? What can we do?"

There was no answer to this appeal. The blanched faces of the listeners showed that all understood the horror of the situation.

Number Fourteen, the passenger train that had just left, was bowling leisurely along at thirty miles an hour, crowded with passengers. Behind, and coming with resistless force, was a runaway engine and three cars, running sixty miles an hour, and behind that train was the heavy broken section, ten loaded stockcars, coming almost as fast.

There seemed to be no hope for the doomed passengers, since on the westbound track the general manager's through express was approaching. To attempt to switch the runaway engine or section would be likely to tear up the track, and the chances were that the loss of life would be just as great, if not greater, than to let the engine speed on its way. No wonder the men turned pale as they grasped the significance of the telegraphed message. No wonder the stoutest hearts stood still, for as they reflected, horror seemed to pile on horror.

Then, out of the gloom there came a steady voice: it seemed filled with an inspiration. It was an opportunity for the genius of a true "railroad man," and the man, or rather boy, was there, ready to prove his capacity.

The boy Tom spoke up: "All of you men get out and oil the track—pour on oil, put on grease, smear it with tallow, or anything! That will slow the engine a little—perhaps enough. After the engine has passed, keep on with the work. Remember we've got to save Flynn's life—yes, and save the cattle too."

The men at once ran out of the depot, Fred and Bob leading all the rest.

"Now, I must save Number Fourteen!" said Tom to himself. "I'll have to keep the westbound track clear and then switch Number Fourteen on to it at Lewistown."

With steady fingers he grasped the telegraph key, and this message flew along the wire:

Operator, Mount Vernon: Flag special train of general manager, and tell him to wait for orders. T. M.

Back came the inquiry:

T. M., Wayville: Who has right to stop special? Track has been cleared for the general manager's train. By whose orders shall I tell him he has been flagged?

It was no time to stick at trifles or to make explanations, so Tom flashed back the answer:

By orders of president of the U.S.R.R., per T. M.

"OK," answered Mount Vernon, as a sign that the order was understood and would be obeyed.

"Now to get Number Fourteen switched from the eastbound to the westbound track! There is just a chance." Again he touched the key.

Operator, Lewistown: Turn crossover switch at your station; transfer passenger train No. 14 from eastbound to westbound track, and hold her there until released. T. M.

Then the key ticked in reply:

T. M., Wayville: Track has been cleared for special of general manager. His train approaching from east with regular orders giving right of way. Make your order more definite, and give authority.

As before, Tom was ready and answered:

Operator, Lewistown: President of U.S.R.R. Co. does not have to show authority. Carry out the orders at once. Important. T. M.

"OK," ticked back the reply.

"Now," said Tom to himself, "if I can only delay the engine until Fourteen gets across on the other track, everything will be all right. The poor horses and cattle will have to take their chances. Let's see, Fourteen has been gone fifteen minutes; she is due at Lewistown in thirty minutes. The runaway engine will be here in about five minutes; unless her speed is reduced, the passenger train will be overtaken about five miles this side of Lewistown. There is only one hope now. I must risk it."

Just then the ticket agent, hearing the men hurrying about, came downstairs and asked about the trouble. As briefly as he could, Tom told him the situation, and then said, "Mr. Lenox, I'm going to climb into the runaway engine, if it's possible, and check her up. I've five dollars or so here. Take it, and if I'm hurt, give it to my mother. Tell her I was going to get her a Christmas present, and tell her I know she would tell me to do just what I'm going to do. God bless her! If I come out all right—and there is a chance—don't ever let her know what I did. Promise, quick!"

"Don't think of such a thing, Tom," pleaded the agent. "Why, it's suicide! If you can slow down the engine, when you get aboard, the rear section will run into you and crush you. If you can't, you are sure to run into the passenger train and die in the collision. In this fog, even if you do get control of the engine—and I doubt if you can—you cannot tell at what second you'll run into the passenger train or what second the other section will be upon you. You are the only support of your mother. Just as likely as not, you'll be killed in your attempt to get on the engine. No one ever got on an engine going as fast as this one is; why, to try it is worse than suicide! Then the engine might blow up. You must not attempt it!"

"That's all very true, Mr. Lenox; but it's better to try, even if I fail, when so many lives will be lost unless an effort is made to save them. I'm going to do all I can, and as for Mother— why, God bless her! Goodbye. I must get out on the platform to be ready."

"Goodbye, and Heaven help you, Tom," replied Mr. Lenox.

Before going out, Tom took off his well-worn overcoat and jacket, tightened his belt, and prepared to run the race of his life. He then went out to the platform and found that the men had oiled the track thoroughly for several hundred yards. He did not dare tell them of his purpose for fear they would stop him, but he said to Bob, "After the engine passes, get all the men you can at work—more are coming every minute. Put on all the oil you can, and tallow, but be careful to see that there is nothing to make the cars jump the track, for that would kill all the cattle and horses, and perhaps poor Jack Flynn! He was seen clinging to the last car at Rockville. But he dared not climb up or jump off, it seems, on account of the speed of the train. There she comes now—I can hear her! I'll run up to the other end of the platform to meet her."

The engine could be heard thundering down the track long before she could be seen coming through the fog. Tom was at the far end of the depot where the men had first begun to apply the oil and grease, and, as they had worked back, he was in a position to get all the benefit of the loss of speed in consequence. The men flew back from the track. When the engine struck the oiled rails she trembled, and her wheels slipped rather than revolved along the track. The momentum was so great that at first the speed was scarcely affected, but as successive sections of track were passed, there began to be quite a marked reduction in speed. Tom noticed this with joy.

The engine was coming rapidly toward him. He turned and ran along the platform in the same direction as the engine, at a speed that would have carried him fifty yards in about six seconds. The engine gained on him, and just as the step was passing, he reached up, grasped the handles, and swung himself up on the step. He rested there for a few seconds and then climbed slowly up into the cab. His face was as white as the card on the steam gauge, and, in spite of the cold wind that blew upon him, he was dripping with perspiration.

Tom glanced up at the gauge and saw that the supply of steam was being rapidly exhausted, and, to his horror, he understood that the engine was running by its own inertia down the steep grade. He closed the throttle, set the lever one notch on the reverse side, and then tried the air brake. It worked in a feeble way, but checked the engine very little. He realized that in order to gain control of the engine he must get up more steam and get the air pump running.

Tom slowly crept along the flying engine over the tender and was pleased to find that there was plenty of water in the tank. Being as strong a fifteen-year-old as one ever sees, he had no trouble in getting up a brisk fire. He then went back to the engine and was gratified to see the steam was rapidly coming up. There was no thought of fear in the brave boy, but he did not forget he was "between two fires." He must keep his own engine from running into the passenger train, and he must keep ahead and out of the way of the runaway section. Anxiously he peered out into the fog, but he could see nothing of the train he was pursuing and could hear nothing of the train that was pursuing him. On sped the flying steed of steel, and still the pointer on the steam gauge moved slowly upward. Twenty pounds more pressure, and he felt he would have complete control of the engine. He was using but little steam now—only enough to try the air pump now and then. In a few moments he moved back the lever another notch toward the reverse and cautiously pulled out the throttle a little. The effect was positive, and he knew he was gaining control of the engine, but how she flew along over culvert, bridge, and trestle, like a living human being on a wild holiday!

Out came the throttle a little farther, and back went the lever another notch. The engine was running slower. "By reversing her and putting on the 'emergency air,' " Tom said to himself, "I can now stop her in three or four lengths. It would be a bad thing to do, but I'll do it if I have to." He looked up at the clock. "In five minutes more, Number Fourteen will have passed to the other track and the switch will be closed. I'll slow up a bit." And so he did.

The engine promptly responded, and settled down to a forty-mile gait. Tom, with his head far out of the window, with one hand on the throttle and the other on the air lever, tried to pierce the mist with those bright dark eyes, but in vain. *Boom!* A torpedo[1] exploded under the wheels. "Number Fourteen has stopped to switch!" said Tom. *Boom! Boom!* Again came the warning torpedoes. " 'Run slowly, with the engine under full control'; that's what those mean." Suddenly Tom's attention was called to a thundering sound from the rear.

"It's the broken section coming like a whirlwind. Now I'm in for it. If she will hold off for two minutes, I'll be all right." Tom threw the lever full ahead and opened the throttle; the engine seemed to leap forward. In a minute more he caught just a glimpse of the rear lights on the passenger train, and knew that a minute later he would be upon her. Nearer came the thundering roar behind him, and he dared not look back. The light in front swerved to the left. Would the switch be closed in time for him to keep ahead of the pursuing section? This was the question which flew through his brain. His engine was at the switch, and it had just been replaced! "Thank God for that!" was the brief prayer he murmured. "The passenger train is safe, if my orders have been carried out. Now to save myself and the cattle behind me. It's a race for life, and I ought to win."

A straight section of track twelve miles long lay before him, with a gently descending grade, then a level mile, and then a four-mile upgrade into Mount Vernon. Once more he crept back to the tender, opened wide the furnace doors, raked the fire, and threw in the coal evenly over every part of the great firebox. He left the ashpit door open for better draft and then climbed up on the coal to see if he could distinguish his relentless pursuer. The light had begun to dispel the fog, and three hundred feet away he could see the oncoming train. *It will take all the speed she's got*, he thought, and leaving the tender, he crept back into the cab.

He opened the throttle wide, pushing the lever over for-

---

1. A detonating device fastened to the top of a rail to be exploded by the pressure of a locomotive or car to give an audible signal to members of a train crew.

ward as far as it would go. The steam kept up, and the only thing to fear was that the axle boxes would get heated on account of the frightful speed of the engine.

But then he reflected that the pace would tell on the freight train's axles even more, since they were not geared to as high a speed as were those of the locomotive.

The engine was now going at the rate of a mile a minute or faster. More coal was necessary, and he resolved to leave the window and stand by the furnace. In ten minutes the level was struck, and the pursuer had gained two hundred feet, on account of its greater weight; a minute later the upgrade was reached. More coal was needed, and the shovel was kept busy feeding the fiery mouth whose tongues of flame seemed never to be satisfied. As the engine began the ascent of the upgrade, the freight section was only fifty feet away. After a mile on the grade, the locomotive pulled slowly away from the freight. Then Tom closed the ashpit door, went back to the window, closed the throttle a little, tried the air brakes, and three minutes later pulled into the depot at Mount Vernon, and came to a stop. He looked out the window, perched high in the air, and said to the operator: "Just wire Wayville that Engine Three-oh-three has arrived here safely, and that Tom's all right."

The crowd of people who were on the platform surrounding the general manager's special car looked with amazement on the young engineer seated in the cab of the smoking engine. The general manager himself was not pleased at the sight, nor at the "unaccountable delay caused by some drunken operator," as he thought, who had imagined he was the president of the road. He had not yielded with the best grace to the order stopping his train and would not have heeded it but for the information that the same person had ordered the eastbound passenger train over to the westbound track, and his order had been obeyed, thus blocking the way. This passenger train might now pull in at any minute. The operator could not get any reply from Wayville to find out about the order.

"Well, young man," said the manager, "what are you doing up in that engine? Don't you know it's against orders? Where are the engineer and fireman? It makes no difference—they are discharged. Get down out of there! Where did you steal the engine?"

Tom could say nothing, but he did not move.

"Be lively there," continued the manager in a rage. "Officer, arrest that boy for stealing the engine!"

"Grandpa, give him a chance to explain," said a young girl who stood near the angry official. "He doesn't look as if he'd stolen anything," she continued.

"I'll attend to him, Mary. He will have a chance to explain in court!"

"Please don't have him arrested," pleaded the young girl—and she seemed to be the only one who dared address her grandfather.

"My dear child, you don't understand these matters. Officer, get this fellow out of there. The engine looks as if it has been badly used."

The officer climbed up into the cab and roughly shook Tom by the shoulder. Tom seemed dazed. What a fate, after all he had braved and done—to be received, instead of with thanks and praise, with threats of arrest and imprisonment!

"Come, get out of here—lively," said the officious policeman, anxious to show his authority before so high an official as the general manager of the U.S.R.R. Co. "You look to me like a pretty tough customer."

This roused Tom's ire.

"Don't touch me, please; I'll get down myself. I want to say just a word to Mr. Holmes." He walked up to that official and said, "I did not steal your engine, and—"

"I don't care to hear any talk," said the manager.

"I don't care to talk, either," said Tom, "but you'd better send the engine back to the grade, and see what's become of Jack Flynn. He was clinging to the rear car of a runaway section of train Number Thirty-three."

"What do you say? The train broken in two? Where did it happen?" asked Mr. Holmes, all interest at once.

"At Cantwell. The train broke in two places coming down the grade. The engine was struck by the flying center section, hurling the engine crew off and starting the engine the other way. I climbed on the runway engine at Wayville and brought her here. The rest of the train is back about two miles—unless she has run back down to the level."

"That's a pretty story. How did you pass Number Fourteen?" asked the manager sternly, after thinking a moment.

"She was switched to the westbound track at Lewistown," answered Tom.

"Tell the engineer and fireman on Thirty-nine to get up in this engine and run her back," said the manager to the conductor. "Officer, you bring the boy along, and I'll go with you. If his story is true, he can go; but if not, it will be all the harder for him."

The trainmen soon had the engine oiled up, finding it was none the worse for its fast run and that Tom had left everything in shipshape order. After they backed down about two miles, a man was seen running up the track. As the engine came nearer, Tom cried out, "It's Jack Flynn—he's all right!"

Sure enough it was Flynn, but he was picked up more dead than alive. No one had ever taken or perhaps will ever take a ride like his. Briefly he told the story of the breaking of the train into three parts—an almost unheard-of thing. He'd been on the center section, alone; he had tried to apply the brakes, but the section he was on collided with the first section. He was thrown down on the top of a car, but had retained his senses enough to cling on. Then he had attempted to climb down on the last car, and drop off, but the speed had been so great he knew the fall would be fatal, and so he had clung to the rear car, expecting death at any moment. But the train came to an upgrade, and the speed had been so reduced that he managed to climb up and set two of the brakes, but then he had to stop. The train gained in speed as it passed the downgrade, and he was glad to climb back again to his old place at the rear of the last car. Next the brakes had parted, and it seemed as if he were rushing to swift destruction. At last, the upgrade being reached, the cars lost speed; he could then have stepped off, but he resolved to stay on until the train stopped, because it was his duty. Just before the cars started to run back to the level, he had dragged a tie across the track and held the section.

"You can 'lay off' until New Year's Day," said Mr. Holmes, after Flynn had finished his story. The engine had by this time stopped in front of the section of the stock train. The cars were coupled on, and a few minutes later the whole train pulled into the depot at Mount Vernon.

The officer by this time had decided not to put the handcuffs on Tom.

"Officer, you can let that boy go," gruffly ordered Mr. Holmes. "Who are you?" he asked Tom.

"I am Thomas Martin's son," he answered. "He used to run the engine of your special—Thirty-nine."

"I thought I'd seen you before. Go into my car and get warm. I see you have neither coat nor overcoat on, and this is a pretty cold day. Mary, get my overcoat and put it on that boy as soon as you can and see that he gets a warm place; he is nearly frozen." Tom was a little abashed as he walked into the magnificent private car of the general manager, escorted by that official's granddaughter. But he was soon at ease and warmly wrapped in a big ulster.

Mr. Holmes went into the telegraph office and directed that the passenger train held at Lewistown should be switched back to its own track and started on its way.

He asked the operator at Wayville who had sent from that office the messages stopping his train, and by whose orders. No one at Wayville was in the office when the dispatches were sent, and no copy of the messages could be found. The operator had been greasing the track and had supposed Tom was similarly employed, as on account of the fog he couldn't tell the men apart.

"That's very strange," muttered Mr. Holmes, as he entered his car and signaled the engineer to go ahead. He was an honest, high-principled man, quick in his methods—the first to see a wrong, the first to right it. He was stern in all his dealings with his men, but he was also just, and they all respected him. He came back to where Tom was seated and said, "Well,

my young engineer, how are you coming on, and where do you want to get off?"

"I'm all right, and I want to get off at Wayville. The mail must be at the station, and I have to take it over to town."

"George," said Mr. Holmes to his son, who was the trainmaster of the road. "Do you happen to remember where the president is today?"

"I think he is in New York."

"Well, I wonder who sent these messages," said Mr. Holmes, handing them over to his son.

Tom flushed, but said nothing.

"They were sent from Wayville, by some man who must have had the running of the trains at his fingers' ends. A train dispatcher could have done no better. I don't know of any man at Wayville who could do it. Do you, Tom?" asked the trainmaster.

"Well, I don't think it was very much of a thing, only a fellow had to think pretty quick."

"Did *you* do it?" asked the general manager suddenly.

"Yes, sir, I did."

"You sent the messages?"

"Yes, sir."

"Are you—besides being a fireman and an engineer—a train dispatcher and operator?"

"And president for an hour," chimed in Mary.

"Yes, sir; I plead guilty to all. But I was only acting president," said Tom.

"How *dared* you do such a thing?" asked Mr. Holmes.

"I dared do anything that would save human life. If someone had not dared, what would have happened? There was but one thing to do, and I did the best I could."

"You are not working for the company?"

"No, sir."

"Would you like to be?"

"Yes, sir."

"George, see that Tom Martin is put on the rolls at fifty dollars a month, as messenger in the general manager's office. His salary began on December first, and he reports for duty on January second."

"Thank you, sir," said Tom heartily.

* * * * *

When the train pulled in at Wayville, there was a large crowd at the depot, and Tom was greeted with cheers as he stepped from the private car. He immediately threw the mail pouches into the handcart that was standing near, and, without saying a word, started to fulfill his duty. Duty was always first with him.

The general manager and his guests got off the train, and, mingling with the crowd, soon learned all that Tom had done in saving the train. They also learned, as they had already guessed, that he was brave, honest, and generous.

The story of his father's death and the struggle of Tom and his mother to save their little home, found many listeners.

In the depot, Mr. Lenox, the ticket agent, was telling Mr. Holmes the whole story over again—of the money Tom had saved to buy a present for his mother, of his last request as he started for the flying engine. Tears stood in both men's eyes as the recital was finished.

"Saved hundreds of lives and untold thousands of dollars by his practical knowledge. A wide-awake boy—fearless and true. Risked his own life—a thorough American boy. I like him,"

said the general manager to the agent, in his crisp, short way.

Then the special train pulled out of the depot, but Tom was not forgotten by its passengers, as the sequel will show.

* * * * *

Christmas Day dawned bright and fair on all the world, yet there was a peculiar brightness and happiness around Tom Martin's home. Tom had purchased a rocking chair for his mother with the money he had earned and was contented with the past and hopeful for the future.

At ten o'clock "Doc" Wise, the express messenger, delivered a large box to Widow Martin's home, and Tom, with all the curiosity of a wide-awake boy, soon had it open. There was a beautiful cloak from Mrs. Holmes for his mother; there was an overcoat and suit of clothes for Tom, given by George Holmes. There was a gold watch from the general manager, bearing the inscription: "He risked his life for others. December 14, 1891." Then there was a check to pay off the mortgage from Mr. Holmes and his guests. Last of all in a pretty frame was a little painting of the runaway engine, No. 303, on which Tom had taken his momentous ride. On the back of the picture was this inscription: "Be always brave and true, and you may indeed be president. Mary Holmes." Of all the presents, Tom liked this one best.

In the evening came the men from the depot, bearing various gifts. It was a fit crowning of a happy day for Tom, because of the knowledge that he had the affection and respect of those who had known him always.

Kane and Pard

Addison Howard Gibson

Life was tough for the little boy: his parents dead—and Uncle Hi too. No one anywhere wanted him or his beloved dog, Pard.

And that snowstorm in the Rockies, from all appearances, would bring closure to both of their young lives.

* * * * *

Here we are, Pard," observed Kane Osborne, looking regretfully after the receding train that had just left him at the isolated mountain station.

Pard, a bright-eyed, alert Scotch collie, glanced up intelligently into the troubled face of his companion, a slender lad of fifteen.

Kane shivered in the chill December air, which swept down from the snow-clad peaks, and his somewhat pale face expressed disappointment as he looked up and down the seemingly deserted station platform.

"No one to meet us, Pard," he said to the tail-wagging collie. "Maybe he don't want us—he didn't write that he did, but Uncle Hi was sure he'd take us in. It's Christmas Eve, and we're all alone, Pard," and Kane swallowed hard as his hand stroked the dog's head. A sympathetic whine was Pard's response.

"Looking for someone, son?" asked the station agent, coming forward.

"Yes," answered Kane, rather bashfully, "we're looking for Mr. Jim Moreley."

"Relation of his going up to the ranch to spend Christmas?"

"No-o-o. Is his ranch near here?"

"About ten miles up Rainbow Canyon," the agent informed him, eyeing the boy. "Moreley hasn't been down today. Going up for a vacation?"

"To live there, if he'll keep us," replied Kane.

"Haven't you any other place to go but to Moreley's ranch?" inquired the agent.

"No place. My folks are all dead, and Uncle Hi died too, about five days ago," explained Kane, trying bravely to hold back the tears. "There's just Pard and me left. A lady offered me a home, but she wouldn't let Pard stay. Uncle Hi used to know Mr. Moreley over at Green Buttes, before he came here, so he got the doctor to write that he was sending Pard and me up to the ranch."

"If you go to live with old Moreley, he'll work you to death," declared the man. "He's changed since he lived at Green Buttes. He's drinking these days, and he's hard on his help. He hasn't any use for anyone who's not strong." He scanned Kane's thin arms and legs in his worn suit.

"Oh, I'll be all right when I get to knocking about the mountains," Kane hastened to assure the agent, resenting the suggestion of physical weakness. "Uncle Hi," he continued, "was sick nearly four months, and I was shut up taking care of him and missed my exercise. Before he died, he told me to come up to Rainbow Canyon. He was sure Mr. Moreley'd be glad to have a boy and a good dog to help with the sheep. I've worked on a sheep ranch before, and Pard knows a lot about the business."

"Well, I'm sorry for you, kid, if you're going up to old Moreley's. Wait a minute." And the agent stepped to the other end of the platform and called to an old man who was unhitching his team from a post in front of a little store near by.

"Hello, Thompson! Here's a boy who wants to go up to Moreley's ranch. Can you give him a lift as far as your place?"

"Guess so, if he's spry," the rancher called back in a crisp tone. "I'm in a hurry!" he explained, climbing into his wagon and gathering up the lines. "There's a storm brewin' in the mountains, and my sheep are scattered in the canyon."

"All right! Here's the boy," said the agent. "Goodbye, kid, and a Merry Christmas to you!"

"Thank you—the same to you!" returned Kane, hurrying toward Thompson's wagon, Pard following closely at his heels.

"Here, kid!" called the agent, running after Kane with an old overcoat. "Put this on. You'll need it riding up Rainbow. You needn't mind returning it—it's too small for me now."

This unexpected kindness brought a lump to Kane's throat, but he murmured his thanks as he slipped into the overcoat. Then he climbed into the wagon. Somewhat impatiently, Thompson moved over in his seat to make room for the unwelcome passenger. He puckered his brows into a frown as his sharp gray eyes ran over the boy critically.

"I'm in a rush," he asserted,

starting his ponies off briskly up the mountain road.

"Got a dog, I see," he remarked presently, with something like a sniff, as Pard trotted along by the wagon. "That feller's attached himself to this outfit with a mighty important air. I ain't got no use for dogs ever since Bill Stevens's killed some o' my lambs. They're a right smart of a nuisance—same as boys. Boys ask too many questions and stand around and watch the old men do the work. I had one from Denver, but he was no good, and I shipped him back. Gid ap, Popcorn!" he said to one of the ponies. "I had a boy o' my own once," his tone softening as he became reminiscent. "But pneumony took him off—pneumony goes hard up here in the Colorado Rockies. Sairy, my wife, is always at me to get a boy to live with us, but after my experience with 'Denver,' no boys for me. No sir, never ag'in!"

Kane felt very uncomfortable as Thompson delivered himself of this speech. At first he stole only a timid, sidelong glance at the man who had no use for boys and dogs. But presently, gathering courage, he surveyed his companion's care-lined face. He decided that Thompson was not as unkind as his words might imply.

"Moreley some connection of

28

yours?" he asked Kane, after driving for some time in silence.

"No," answered Kane, snuggling his chin down inside the turned-up collar of his newly acquired overcoat. "Uncle Hi thought Pard and I might find a job there."

"Who's Uncle Hi?"

"A kind old man I lived with after my father and mother died."

"Why didn't you stay with him?" Thompson asked, darting a suspicious glance at Kane from under a ledge of bushy brows.

"He died too, and it took everything to pay the funeral expenses. Dr. Bentley paid my way up to Rainbow. When I earn money enough, I'll pay him back and buy a tombstone for Uncle Hi."

"Well, lad, it's a world o' trouble!" The old man sighed deeply. "I was gittin' along tip-top till our boy died. After that I seemed to run downhill and had to mortgage my ranch to Jim Moreley to keep goin'. But," pridefully, "I got some fine sheep, and if I've good luck winterin' 'em, I'll pay out next fall, and be independent ag'in."

As they steadily ascended, the wind grew more chilly and moaned ominously among the pines that dotted the mountain slopes. The keen air made Kane's nose and ears tingle, and he drew closer to his companion.

"Goin' to storm," observed Thompson, squinting toward the sky. "It's a sure sign when the pines screech that way. Here we are," he announced, turning off on a side trail. "That's my place," pointing to a homey-looking cottage that stood in a sheltered arm of the wide canyon.

"It's about three miles up the trail yonder to Moreley's," he explained. "You can eat a bite with Sairy and me before goin' on."

As Kane helped unhitch the ponies, a motherly look-ing woman called from the house that dinner was ready. She made friends with Pard at once and brought him a plate of scraps from the kitchen.

"Some Christmas fixin's for you, Sairy," said Thompson, as he and Kane deposited on the table several packages brought from Rainbow.

In the neat, warm kitchen, Kane, seated between the old couple, ate his share of the good "boiled dinner" with a gusto caused by a keen appetite. More than once he caught Mrs. Thompson's kindly eyes fixed on his face with an almost yearning eagerness.

The meal over, Pard had another feast in the shed behind the kitchen. Then, thanking the couple for their kindness, Kane slipped into the overcoat and prepared for his climb up to Moreley's ranch.

"He reminds me so much of Harry," Kane overheard Mrs. Thompson say in an undertone to her husband. "Why can't we keep him? Moreley's will be such a rough place for him."

Thompson muttered something about boys and dogs be-ing a great deal of bother.

"It seems as if Providence sent him to us," she persisted, "your bringing him here, and on Christmas Eve too! He's like a Christmas present," with a smile directed at Kane. Then, with a pleading quiver of the pleasant voice, "Do let's keep him—and that fine collie!"

But Thompson shook his head decisively.

"Well, we can at least keep him overnight—Christmas Eve," she pleaded. "It's three o'clock now, and these short days it gets dark so early in the mountains. It's going to storm soon," looking out the window, "and the trail being strange to him, he might miss his way."

"The trail's all right if he follows it," declared the old rancher impatiently. "He'd best go on, for Moreley's a crank and might think we're tryin' to coax the boy from goin' to him."

From the foot of the steep trail Kane waved his hand to Mrs. Thompson, as she stood in the doorway watching him start off.

"So much like Harry," she murmured tremulously. "God guard him!"

"Just stick to that trail, and it'll lead you straight to Moreley's," directed Thompson, calling after Kane. "Don't waste any time, though. See that cloud rolling over Old Grayback?" indicating a peak. "That means a snowstorm, and my sheep are scattered somewhere in the canyon. I've got to hustle."

Kane turned to offer the services of Pard and himself to help round up the sheep, but Thompson had hurried away and disappeared down the canyon. So he went on up the trail. To reinforce his courage, he began to whistle, but something in his throat choked him, and he became thoughtful.

"Pard," gently squeezing the collie's ear, "if Mr. Moreley don't want us, we'll be in a fix." A rapid movement of the tail and a low whine attested to Pard's loyal sympathy.

The cloud over Old Grayback soon obscured the entire sky. Presently Kane felt fine particles of snow strike his face, and the path became slippery and difficult to follow.

"This is going back two steps to one forward, Pard!" he laughed, recovering from measuring his full length on an icy rock.

The wind, accompanied by a steadily falling temperature, increased in power every minute, driving the now rapidly descending snow before it. Kane pulled his cap down to protect his eyes and struggled on.

Suddenly Kane realized he had strayed from the trail and was stumbling along half blindly down a canyon over rocks and tangled bushes. Here the trees broke the fierce, biting force of the wind. But he had no idea which way to turn to find the path that he had lost. All around and enwrapping him was a mass of roaring, smothering whiteness.

Kane had lived most of his years among the Rockies, but he had never before been lost in one of these wild winter storms. He knew, however, that his situation was one of great danger. Unless he could find shelter, he might become buried under the snow or stumble over a ledge into an unseen gorge. Then there might be a terrible snowslide from the overladen heights above. He could see scarcely ten yards in any direction, and in spite of the overcoat, he began to feel chilled. He was now so weary he felt the urge to crawl under the shelving rocks and lie down.

Realizing how fatal such a step might prove, Kane fought his way across the snow-clad canyon, followed by Pard.

All at once the collie gave a sharp bark and darted away through the trees, reappearing almost immediately and barking up at Kane as if insisting on his following.

"All right, Pard. Lead on!" directed Kane.

Only a short distance farther, a long shed loomed vague and specterlike in the wild whiteness of the evening. Pushing forward, Kane discovered it was a rude, but comfortable building for stock. It stood in an arm of the canyon with no house in sight.

Thankful for anything that promised refuge from the storm, he advanced hurriedly. At the corner of the building, he halted quickly: a herd of sheep huddled against the closed door.

Kane's appearance was greeted by a plaintive chorus of bleats. In their dumb, beseeching way they accepted him as their belated shepherd.

"All right, sheepsie-baas," he said soothingly as they crowded about him. "Wait, and I'll see how things are."

Sliding back the big door, Kane revealed a warm, comfortable shed for sheep and cattle. In one of the stalls a cow stood munching hay.

"Someone doesn't look after his sheep very well, Pard," said Kane. "Bring 'em in."

The well-trained collie needed no second bidding. With an assenting bark, he ran around the shivering flock, which quickly scattered among the bushes. It proved no easy task to corral these sheep, for, being unused to a dog, the younger ones were frightened and at first fled in every direction. But Kane hurried out to direct matters, and Pard, wise and careful in his part of the business, after considerable effort brought them, an obedient bunch, into their fold. Then their self-appointed shepherd filled the low racks with hay, which they began to eat gratefully.

"Well, Bossy," addressing the cow, "we've invited ourselves to spend Christmas Eve with you and the sheepsie-baas. Here, Pard! Where are you?" he called, noticing that the collie had not entered the shed. Off somewhere in the bushes, Pard began a spirited barking.

Some stubborn runaways, thought Kane. "Bring 'em in, Pard," he commanded over the din of the storm.

Pard sent back a quick, answering bark. Kane repeated his order, and again the collie responded with a sharp, imperative bark. Sure that something was wrong, the boy left the shelter of the shed, and again faced the fury of the elements.

"Where are you, Pard?"

Kane bent his head to listen for the dog's bark to guide him. It came, and was instantly followed by the sound of a groan—a human groan!

Quickly Kane groped his way through the underbrush of the canyon. Guided by Pard's persistent barking, he at last reached an object lying among the rocks and almost buried in snow. A nearer survey revealed a man lying prostrate and helpless in a little clump of bushes.

"I've had a fall and hurt my ankle so I can't walk in the snow!" said the unfortunate man, groaning with pain, as Kane bent solicitously over him.

"Why, it's Mr. Thompson!" cried Kane, in surprise. "How did it happen?"

"In trying to bunch my sheep, I slipped on a rock and took a bad tumble," explained Mr. Thompson. "I dragged myself through the snow as far as these bushes, then my strength gave out. The pain and cold together made me kind of lose my senses, I guess, till the dog roused me."

Half-leading, half-dragging the rancher, Kane managed to get him to the shed. Here, on an improvised couch of hay and empty sacks, the disabled man watched his safely sheltered flock taking their supper in calm content.

"Well, Providence works funny sometimes!" he sighed. "There I was, flounderin' in the snow, disablin' myself and worryin' for fear my sheep'd all perish, and finally realized I was a goner myself. And there you was, losin' the trail all for a purpose—to do my work and save my life."

"It was mostly Pard," asserted Kane, stroking the collie's head. "He drove the sheep in and found you."

"It was the two of you," corrected Thompson, looking gratefully at the boy and his dog. "I'm not harborin' any more prejudices ag'in' boys and dogs—you two in particular. The storm's knocked them prejudices all out o' me. The house is jest round the bend of the canyon. The wind's fallin' now, and purty soon you can go and tell Sairy what's happened. I ain't goin' to let Jim Moreley have you! You and Pard are Christmas presents to Sairy and me!"

In silent thankfulness, Kane, too happy for words, pressed the rancher's hand. Pard only wagged his tail.

In Clean Hay

Eric P. Kelly

Hetman (a military leader): In all your lands there are tidings about a newborn Child. Unknown in what family, yet still a kingly Son. People find in Him a miracle—that he shall be King of the whole world. Ignorant peasant folk are collecting and seek Him everywhere in the kingdom, and then too, some of the nobles are even seeking to honor Him and put their trust in Him.

Herod: I heard all that from Three Kings who were here, but I don't know where the Child is.

Hetman: King, in Bethlehem City, He is born, and lies in a stable in clean hay.—From Szopka Krakowska, "Krakow Stable," a miracle play performed these seven hundred years in the streets of Krakow, Poland.

* * * * *

Without question, Poland's greatest contribution to the Christmas season is the Szopka. Eric P. Kelly, author of The Trumpeter of Krakow, *in this story depicts two sets of Szopka performers, one doomed to heartbreak.*

Unless . . .

* * * * *

In a little village on the outskirts of the Polish city of Krakow there stands a happy farmhouse whose owner is Pan Yan. In the early spring, the fields about the house are dark and rich, awaiting the planting of seed, and in the summer they are green with ripened grain. In the fall they turn to russet brown, and in the winter they lie deep beneath the shining snow. From earliest morning until sundown, the house is astir with action, but at sundown everything ceases, and peace descends, for did the Lord not ordain that all work should cease with the sun? Then the lamp is lighted in the large room, and the newspaper, which has come from Krakow, will be read to all the family by the father or the eldest boy, Antek. The others sit about and listen. Antek is fifteen and goes every day to the high school in the city; it is a walk of about three miles, but the road is good, and there is often company on the way.

Antek reads from the gazette: "Tomorrow is the day before Christmas and there will be many visitors who come to the city to attend services at night in the churches. The Christmas trees will be on sale in the *rynek* [marketplace], and the booths, full of candy and toys, will be opened directly after dark. In the homes, the children will await the sight of the first star. When the first star shines, then an angel will come and knock at the door, and the rejoicing at the birth of Christ will begin. This year there will be a special treat for Krakow people, for a very famous performer will give his puppet play, the *Szopka Krakowska*, at the Falcon's Hall on Grodzka Street. With him will be his wife, who will sing the hymns."

Antek put down the paper. "Our puppet show is all made."

The father: "Don't stay out too late."

Antek answered quickly, "No, Father, we won't. We will give our show several times between five and seven o'clock, and then we will start on the road home."

In one corner of the little farmhouse stood a small, wooden two-towered church in miniature; between the towers at the base, large doors stood wide open, revealing a stage. And on this stage were piled a number of little wooden figures, like dolls dressed in various jaunty colors, and in the background was the figure of a woman with a baby in her arms. This was a stage in miniature—a *Szopka Krakowska* with its little wooden puppets. When set up for the entertainment of onlookers, Antek would crawl beneath it and operate the puppets from little sticks that went through a slot in the floor. This slot extended the whole length of the stage, so that a puppet could be brought upon the scene from one side, made to perform, and then be taken away on the farther side. During the performance of a puppet play, the figures moved in constant succession across this stage.

The mother entered from the stove-room with a huge pot of steaming soup and poured it out into wooden bowls before each of the children.

"Well, tomorrow will be Christmas Eve," she said, "and you will go out with the *Szopka*."

"Yes. And make a lot of money." This was from Stefan, the second in age. He was a more practical boy than his brother, although younger—yet he had less of the vivid imagination which made Antek the better showman of the puppet show.

The mother sighed. "I wish we could give it to you, but what we have is being set aside for the days when you go up to the university. How much did you make last year?"

"Fifty zlotys," [about ten dollars], answered Antek proudly.

"We'll make a hundred this year," said Stefan.

"And what will you do with it?" asked the mother.

A clamor went up. Antek was saying something about a book, Stefan about a chest of tools, and Anusia, the "baby"

of ten years, said something that sounded like "shoes." Christopher, who played all the songs for the *Szopka* on his violin, tried to make known his want for new strings and a bow. However, the whole pandemonium was such that anyone might see that at least *something* was wanted rather eagerly. It was true, as the mother had said, that the scanty profits from the farm were going into the children's educations: Antek for the university, Stefan for the School of Commerce and Trade, Christopher for the Academy of Music, and Anusia for—well that would come later. The child had a clear, appealing voice and might become a great singer if placed with the proper teachers. Who knows?

Therefore this chance of making a little money on the night before Christmas meant a great deal to them all. The boys, working with the father, had built the little theater themselves. It stood upon little folding legs which Stefan had devised. The mother had dressed the dolls, and on the night before Christmas, it was all in readiness to carry to Krakow. Now, since the very earliest days of the city, boys have gone about in Krakow giving this show on Christmas Eve, most of them poor or needy boys to whom the gift of money was a veritable godsend. And on Christmas Eve there descends over the earth, each year, that spirit of gladness and kindness that makes people eager and anxious to relieve suffering and soften the hard ways of life with the cheer that the Christ child brought to men.

The day before Christmas dawned bright. It was crisp but not so cold as usual. There was not a cloud in the sky, and the children knew that they could not have selected a better day for their puppet show. At about one o'clock in the afternoon they started for Krakow. Antek walked in front with the *Szopka* strapped to his shoulders. Stefan, carrying the sticks on which the *Szopka* was to rest, walked by his side. Christopher

on the left side, carrying his violin and bow in a case in one hand, had extended the other hand to Anusia, who walked just beyond. A happy company it was, and all along the way people greeted them and shouted out *"Wesolych Swiat!"* [Merry Christmas!] Or else *"Niech Bedzie Pochwalony Jesus Christ."* [May Jesus Christ be praised.] As they neared the city, the sun was sinking, for they had walked slowly and too, the sun sinks early in the Christmas season. Lights were coming on everywhere, and as they stood at the Florian Gate, Anusia turning about, screamed with delight, and pointed at the sky.

For there, hanging like a little candle, was the first star. The Christmas season had begun.

* * * * *

In the marketplace they selected a corner by one path and mounted the puppet theater on its legs. "It was here that we stood last year," said Antek.

Candles were lighted before the little theater; a crowd gathered. Then Anusia stepped out before the people and bravely sang a little carol, while Christopher played on the violin. The crowd increased.

"Oh, what a crowd!" cried Stefan, rubbing his hands. "Here, at least for the first performance, is a good twenty-five zlotys." His words were correct. The first performance netted exactly that amount. It was a splendid performance too—Anusia sang the carols beautifully, Antek made the puppets dance as if they were alive, and everybody reached for handkerchiefs when King Herod ordered that all the babies in the kingdom should be put to death.

They had begun again when suddenly there came a rude end to their performance—and to all their hopes.

A dignitary wearing a huge star stepped into the circle

before the little theater and ordered the play to be stopped.

"We can't! We can't!" shrieked Stefan, who was reading the lines for the puppets. "Don't bother us. The show must go on."

The dignitary grinned. "Where is your license?" he asked.

"License?" Antek crept out from beneath the theater where he was operating the puppets and faced the officer.

"Yes. Don't you know that you must buy a license to give public performances in this city?"

"No. It was not so last year."

"But it is so this year. It is a new ordinance that no shows may be given on the streets without a license."

"How much is the license?" asked Antek.

"One hundred zlotys," said the man.

"But I haven't got one hundred zlotys!" groaned Antek.

"Then you must move along or I will report you to the police." He motioned to a police officer on the corner.

"Come quick," ordered Antek, snatching up the theater to his back. "Take the stool, Stefan, and you, Anusia, hang on to Christopher."

They emerged in a quiet place behind the Cloth Hall to take counsel.

"We can't do anything. We've got to go home," Antek announced. Every face fell. Anusia began to cry. "It can't be helped. We must obey the law, and we haven't one hundred zlotys in the world."

"Let's give the show in some private street," suggested Stefan.

"Can't be done. We'd be arrested."

They marched out into the street. Two men engaged in a spirited conversation almost ran them down.

"Look out there," said one, sidestepping the *Szopka*. "The street doesn't belong to you boys."

"No, but we have our rights," answered Antek.

"That you have," answered the second man, suddenly striking Antek in friendly fashion upon the back. "A *Szopka*, as I live!"

"A *Szopka*—" the second man fell back in amazement.

"Yes, and a good one," said the first man examining the show quickly. "Here is an answer to our prayers sent from Heaven. Do you people operate the *Szopka*?"

"We do," answered Antek wonderingly.

"Do you want an engagement?"

"Yes!" shouted Antek, Stefan, and Christopher at the tops of their voices.

"Then come with us. You see, we were to have had a very famous *Szopka* with us tonight—Pan Kowalski and his wife were to entertain us. The crowd is all there—has been for half an hour—waiting for the show to begin. And there is no Pan Kowalski. We have looked up and down the town; we have hunted all through the villages; we have inquired everywhere that he might have been, and yet we cannot find him. We must have the show or send the people home."

"How much do we get?" asked Stefan, characteristically, for he had recovered from his astonishment at this quick turn of affairs.

"We will take a collection. We can guarantee you at least one hundred zlotys. You will probably make much more than that."

As they spoke, the two men hustled the children along Grodzka Street and stopped in front of a building on which there was a coat of arms bearing the figure of a falcon.

"In here," said one of the men.

"Why this is the Falcon Hall we read of in the newspaper," said Stefan. "This is the best place in Krakow in which to give the *Szopka*. Antek," he turned to his brother, "do you realize that we will make lots of money out of this?"

"We must give a good performance first," admonished Antek.

One of the men made a speech to the people, while the children prepared the show. He was sorry, he said, that Pan Kowalski had not been able to come. But in his place there had come a very fine *Szopka* operated by young men who were quite experienced—at this the crowd laughed, for the youth of the performers was quite evident. "It is Christmas Eve," the man went on. "And it is not the time to show any displeasure. We have come here to see acted the old story of the wonderful evening so many centuries ago when Christ was born on earth to bring peace and goodwill to all men."

It was a Christmas crowd at that, and if it felt any ill will at this substitution on the program, it did not show it. The lamp in front of the stage was lighted. Antek stepped out in front and played on his little bugle the *"Heynal"* or little trumpet song that the trumpeter in the tower of the Church of Our Lady had played every hour of the day and night since Christianity in Krakow began. Then lights appeared in the two towers, and Christopher and Anusia stepped out to play and sing the old hymn, "Amid the Silence." The curtains were swept back by Stefan, and there on the stage were two shepherds sleeping. Red fire burns, an angel descends, and again Christopher and Anusia step forward. This time the song is "Gloria in Excelsis Deo," the song sung by the angels when Christ was born. The curtain is closed. It opens again on Bethlehem, whither the shepherds have come to greet the Christ child, who lies there with the mother, asleep on the clean hay. From the back of the manger, a sheep and a cow look over the wall.

Then the scene changes. We are now in the court of Herod, the king, and Three Kings come in from the East to ask their way to the newborn King. Herod cannot tell them, and so they go out again and follow a star that is gleaming in the heavens; here Stefan lifts into the air a great gold star which shines with brilliance when the light falls upon it. They come to the Christ child, and they, too, worship. Then the shepherds dance, and the soldiers sing, and the violin makes merry music for all the company. It is truly a splendid sight; the children shout, the babies crow, and the men and women clap their hands in applause.

Oh, thou cruel Herod! For now he commands his hetman to send out the soldiers and destroy the Christ child. But because they do not know who the Christ child is, they must destroy every child in the kingdom. Cruel King Herod, for this thou shalt pay—for the floor of the stage opens, and the devil dances out. How the children scream as he cuts off Herod's head, and the head goes rolling out of the little theater and onto the floor.

Then there comes more dancing and singing; little Anusia sings like an angel. The men and women take her up, and the children kiss her and stroke her hands.

And when the collection is taken, the bowl is heaped high with paper and silver and copper. There are at least five hundred zlotys [about one hundred dollars] on the plate—the best day's work that any *Szopka* has ever done in Krakow. The crowd leaves slowly; the men come and take their leave of the children; the show is packed up, and

the four, now beaming with happiness and delight, take again the road for the village three miles away. It is a lovely night, not overly cold, but just comfortably cold; and though there is no moon, the stars are as bright as little pinpoints of light in the *Szopka* walls. As they pass the Church of Our Lady, the children hear the trumpet playing the "Heynal," and it makes them feel suddenly that over all the world has come this happiness at the birth of Christ.

Two hours later, on the road again, they stop at the home of neighbor Kolesza for a rest. He meets them at the door with a Christmas greeting and then tells them to come to the stable for there they will find a surprise.

"I had no room for them in the house," he said. "The hay of the stable is much warmer than my floor, and I have a stove here where I have heat for the animals in winter. Come, and you shall see."

They entered the stable. He flashed his lantern high above his head. They looked; they drew their breaths, and then with one accord fell upon their knees.

For there in the manger was a young woman. She had been sleeping but was now awake, and in her arms, nestled closely to her body, was a little baby, wrapped in a blue coat.

"It is like the Christ child," whispered Stefan. "See, there is the cow and the sheep looking over the back of the manger, and there is the place where the wise men knelt." He pointed. Indeed, a dark figure arose there and looked about; it was a man, and he put his fingers to his lips lest they should talk and disturb the mother and child.

"It is Pan Kowalski, the puppet show man," said Pan Kolesza in an undertone. "He was on his way to Krakow tonight to give a performance in the hall of the falcons. He and his wife stopped here, and while they were here this child was born."

The children looked at each other strangely. Then they looked at Pan Kowalski and then at the mother and the child.

"They have no money," went on Pan Kolesza. "They were to have received much money for their performance in Krakow tonight, but they were not able to go, and therefore they lose it. I do not know what they will do when they leave here, though the good God knows I will let them stay as long as they like. They have only this show which they give at Christmas; it is not given at any other time of the year."

"And it was on this night that Christ was born," said Antek. "Stefan, . . ." he added after a long pause.

"I know what you are going to say," retorted Stefan. They went out into the air again, not even taking leave of either of the men, so engrossed were they in their own thoughts.

"It means that we lose what we wanted," said Antek. "I think I'll go back."

"No," said Stefan. "Let me."

Antek squeezed something into his hand. Stefan ran back to the stable and entered. Pan Kowalski had sunk into a stupor again and heeded nothing; Stefan crept up to the manger and listened to the deep breathing of the mother. Then he slipped his hand over the edge of the manger and dropped all the silver and notes that had been collected in Krakow. Then he fell upon his knees for a moment and said a little prayer. But as he staggered after his companions down the long dark road, something of the most infinite happiness seized upon his heart, and when he reached Antek, he was sobbing like a baby. Whereupon Antek fell to sobbing likewise, and out there upon the Krakow road Christ was born again in the hearts of four happy children.

Where the Christmas Tree Grew

Mary Eleanor Wilkins Freeman

Earl Munroe, son of the richest man in town, lorded over the children attending No. 4 District School. Now, he turned the full force of his personality on eight-year-old Jenny Brown, who wore tattered clothes and shoes and rarely had enough to eat.

Alas! His blandishments worked all too well—Jenny was lost on the snowy mountain!

* * * * *

It was afternoon recess at No. 4 District School, in Warner. There was a heavy snowstorm; so everyone was in the warm schoolroom, except a few adventurous spirits who were tumbling about in the snowdrifts out in the yard, getting their clothes wet and preparing themselves for scoldings at home. Their shrill cries and shouts of laughter floated into the schoolroom, but the small group near the stove did not heed them at all. There were five or six little girls and one boy. The girls, with the exception of Jenny Brown, were trim and sweet in their winter dresses and neat school aprons; they perched on the desks and the arms of the settee with careless grace, like birds. Some of them had their arms linked. The one boy lounged against the blackboard. His dark, straight-profiled face was all aglow as he talked. His big brown eyes gazed now soberly and impressively at Jenny, then gave a merry dance in the direction of the other girls.

"Yes, it does—*honest!*" said he.

The other girls nudged one another softly, but Jenny Brown stood with her innocent, solemn eyes fixed upon Earl Munroe's face, drinking in every word.

"You ask anybody who knows," continued Earl, "ask Judge Barker, ask—the minister—"

"Oh!" cried the little girls, but the boy shook his head impatiently at them.

"Yes," said he, "you just go and ask Mr. Fisher tomorrow, and you'll see what he'll tell you. Why, look here," Earl straightened himself and stretched out an arm like an orator, "it's nothing more than *reasonable* than that Christmas trees grow wild with the presents all on 'em! What sense would there be in 'em if they didn't, I'd like to know? They grow in different places, of course; but these around here grow mostly on the mountain over there. They come up every spring, and they all blossom out about Christmastime, and folks go hunting for them to give to the children. Father and Ben are over on the mountain today."

"Oh, oh!" cried the little girls.

"I mean, I guess they are," amended Earl, trying to put his feet on the boundary line of truth. "I hope they'll find a full one."

Jenny Brown had a little, round, simple face; her thin brown hair was combed back and braided tightly in one tiny braid tied with a bit of shoestring. She wore a nondescript gown, which nearly trailed behind and showed in front her little, coarsely shod feet, which toed in helplessly. The gown was of a faded green color; it was scalloped and bound around

the bottom, and had some green ribbon bows down the front. It was, in fact, the discarded polonaise of a benevolent woman, who aided the poor substantially but not tastefully.

Jenny Brown was eight and small for her age—a strange, gentle, ignorant little creature, never doubting the truth of what she was told, which sorely tempted the other children to impose upon her. Standing there in the schoolroom that stormy recess, in the midst of that group of wiser, richer, mostly older girls, and that one handsome, mischievous boy, she believed every word she heard.

This was her first term at school, and she had never before seen much of other children. She had lived her eight years all alone at home with her mother, and she had never been told about Christmas. Her mother had other things to think about. She was a dull, spiritless, reticent woman, who had lived through much trouble. She worked, doing washings and cleanings, like a poor feeble machine that still moves but has no interest in its motion. Sometimes the Browns had almost enough to eat, at other times they half starved. It was half-starving time just then; Jenny had not had enough to eat that day.

There was a pinched look on the little face upturned toward Earl Munroe's.

Earl's words gained authority by coming from himself. Jenny had always regarded him with awe and admiration. It was much that he should speak at all to her.

Earl Munroe was quite the king of this little district school. He was the son of the wealthiest man in town. No other boy was so well dressed, so gently bred, so luxuriously lodged and fed. Earl himself realized his importance and had, at times, the loftiness of a young prince in his manner. Occasionally, some independent urchin would bristle with democratic spirit and tell him to his face that he was "stuck up" and that he hadn't so much more to be proud of than other folks—that his grandfather wasn't anything but an old ragman!

Then Earl would wilt. Arrogance in a free country is likely to have an unstable foundation. Earl tottered at the mention of his paternal grandfather, who had given the first impetus to the family fortune by driving a tin cart about the country. Moreover, the boy was really pleasant and generous hearted and had no mind, in the long run, for a lonely state and disagreeable haughtiness. He enjoyed being lordly once in a while, that was all.

He did now, with Jenny. He eyed her with a lofty condescension that would have greatly amused his tin-peddler grandfather.

Soon the bell rang. They all filed to their seats, and the lessons were begun.

After school was done that night, Earl stood in the doorway when Jenny passed by.

"Say, Jenny," he called, "when are you going over to the mountain to find the Christmas tree? You'd better go pretty soon or they'll be gone."

"That's so!" chimed in one of the girls. "You'd better go right away, Jenny."

She passed along, her face shyly dimpling with her innocent little smile and said nothing. She would never talk much.

She had quite a long walk to her home. Presently, as she was pushing weakly through the new snow, Earl went flying past her in his father's sleigh, with the black horses and the fur-capped coachman. He never thought of asking her to ride. If he had, he would not have hesitated a second before doing so.

Jenny, as she waded along, could see the mountain always before her. This road led straight to it, then turned and wound around its base. It had stopped snowing, and the sun was setting clear. The great white mountain was all rosy. It stood op-

posite the red western sky. Jenny kept her eyes fixed upon the mountain. Down in the valley shadows, her little simple face, pale and colorless, gathered another kind of radiance.

There was no school the next day, which was the one before Christmas. It was pleasant and not very cold. Everybody was out; the little village stores were crowded. Sleds trailing Christmas greenery went flying; people were hastening with parcels under their arms, their hands full.

Jenny Brown also was out. She was climbing Franklin Mountain. The snowy pine boughs bent so low that they brushed her head; she stepped deeply into the untrodden snow, and the train of her green polonaise dipped into it and swept it along. And all the time she was peering through those white fairy columns and arches for—a Christmas tree.

That night, the mountain had turned rosy and faded, and the stars were coming out when a frantic woman, panting, crying out now and then in her distress, went running down the road to the Munroe house. It was the only one between her own and the mountain. The woman rained some clattering knocks on the door—she could not stop for the bell. Then she burst into the house and threw open the dining room door, crying out in gasps, "Hev you seen her? Oh, hev you? My Jenny's lost! She's lost! Oh, oh, oh! They said they saw her comin' up this way this mornin'. *Hev* you seen her? *Hev* you?"

Earl and his father and mother were having tea there in the handsome oak-paneled dining room. Mr. Munroe rose at once and went forward. Mrs. Munroe looked with a pale face around her silver tea urn, and Earl sat as if frozen. He heard his father's soothing questions and the mother's answers. She had been out at work all day. When she returned, Jenny was gone. Someone had seen her going up the road to the Munroes' that morning about ten o'clock. That was her only clue.

Earl sat there and saw his mother draw the poor woman into the room and try to comfort her. He heard, with a vague understanding, his father order the horses to be harnessed immediately. He watched him putting on his coat and hat out in the hall.

When he heard the horses trot up the drive, he sprang to his feet. When Mr. Munroe opened the door, Earl, with his coat and cap on, was at his heels.

"Why, you can't go, Earl!" said his father, when he saw him. "Go back at once."

Earl was white and trembling. He half sobbed. "Oh, Father, I *must* go!" said he.

"Earl, be reasonable. You want to help, don't you, and not hinder?" his mother called out of the dining room.

Earl caught hold of his father's coat. "Father, look here. *I believe I know where she is!*"

Then his father faced sharply around; his mother and Jenny's stood listening in bewilderment, and Earl told his ridiculous, childish, and cruel little story. "I didn't dream she'd really be such a little goose as to go," he choked out, "but she must have, for," with brave candor, "I know she believed every word I told her."

It seemed a fantastic theory, yet a likely one. It would give method to the search, yet more alarm to the searchers. The mountain was a wide region in which to find one little child.

Jenny's mother screamed out, "Oh, if she's lost on the mountain, they'll never find her! They never will; they never will! Oh Jenny, Jenny, Jenny!"

Earl gave a despairing glance at her and bolted upstairs to his own room. His mother called pityingly after him, but he only sobbed back, "Don't, Mother—please!" and kept on.

The boy, lying face downward on his bed, crying as if his heart would break, heard presently the church bell clang out fast and furious. Then he heard loud voices down in the road and the flurry of sleigh bells. His father had raised the alarm, and the search was organized.

After a while, Earl arose and crept over to the window. It looked toward the mountain, which towered up, cold and white and relentless, like one of the ice-hearted giants of the old Indian tales. Earl shuddered as he looked at it. Presently, he slipped downstairs and into the parlor. In the bay window stood, like a gay mockery, the Christmas tree. It was a quite small one that year, only for the family—some expected guests had failed to come—but it was well laden. After tea, the presents were to have been distributed. There were some for his father and mother and some for the servants, but the bulk of them were for Earl.

By and by, his mother, who had heard him come downstairs, peeped into the room and saw him busily taking his presents from the tree. Her heat sank with sad displeasure and amazement. She would not have believed that her boy could be so utterly selfish as to think of Christmas presents *then*.

But she said nothing. She stole away and returned to poor Mrs. Brown, whom she was keeping with her. Still, she continued to think of it all that long, terrible night when they sat there waiting, listening to the signal horns over on the mountain.

Morning came at last, and Mr. Munroe with it. No success so far. He had a bite to eat and was off again. That was

quite early. An hour or two later, the breakfast bell rang. Earl did not respond to it, so his mother went to the foot of the stairs and called him. There was a stern ring in her soft voice. All the time she had in mind his heartlessness and greediness over the presents. When Earl did not answer, she went upstairs and found that he was not in his room. Then she looked in the parlor and stood staring in bewilderment. Earl was not there, but neither were the Christmas tree and his presents— they had vanished bodily!

Just at that moment Earl Munroe was hurrying down the road, and he was dragging his big sled on which were loaded his Christmas presents and the Christmas tree. The top of the tree trailed in the snow; its branches spread over the sled on either side, and rustled. It was a heavy load, but Earl tugged manfully in an enthusiasm of remorse and atonement—a fantastic, extravagant atonement, planned by that same fertile fancy which had invented that story for poor little Jenny, but instigated by all the good, repentant impulses in the boy's nature.

On every one of those neat parcels, above his own name, was written in his big, crooked, childish hand, "To Jenny Brown, from—" Earl Munroe had not saved one Christmas present for himself.

Pulling the sled along, his cheeks brilliant, his eyes glowing, he met Maud Barker. She was Judge Barker's daughter and the girl who had joined him in advising Jenny to hunt on the mountain for the Christmas tree.

Maud stepped along, placing her trim little feet with dainty precision; she wore some new high-buttoned overshoes. She also carried a new beaver muff, but in one hand only. The other dangled mittenless at her side; it was pink with cold, but on its third finger sparkled a new gold ring with a blue stone in it.

"Oh, Earl!" she called out, "have they found Jenny Brown? I was going up to your house to . . . Why, Earl Munroe, what have you got there?"

"I'm carrying my Christmas presents and the tree up to Jenny's—so she'll find 'em when she comes back," said the boy, flushing red. There was a little defiant choke in his voice.

"Why, what for?"

"I rather think they belong to her, more 'n they do to me, after what's happened."

"Does your mother know?"

"No, but she wouldn't care. She'd think I was only doing what I ought."

"All of 'em?" queried Maud, feebly.

"You don't s'pose I'd keep any back?"

Maud stood staring. It was beyond her comprehension.

Earl was passing on when a thought struck him.

"Say, Maud," he cried eagerly, "haven't you something you can put in? Girls' things might please her better, you know. Some of mine are—rather odd, I'm afraid."

"What have you got?" demanded Maud.

"Well, some of the things are well enough. There's a lot of candy and oranges and figs and books; there's one by Jules Verne I guess she'll like. But there's a great big jackknife, and a brown velvet bicycle suit."

"Why, Earl Munroe! What could she do with a bicycle suit?"

"I thought, maybe, she could rip the seams to 'em an' sew 'em some way, an' get a basque cut, or something. Don't you s'pose she could?" Earl asked, anxiously.

"I don't know; her mother could tell," said Maud.

"Well, I'll hang it on, anyhow. Maud, haven't you anything to give her?"

"I . . . don't know."

Earl eyed her sharply. "Isn't that muff new?"

"Yes."

"And that ring?"

Maud nodded.

"She'd be delighted with 'em. Oh, Maud, put 'em in!"

Maud looked at him. Her pretty mouth quivered a little, some tears twinkled in her blue eyes.

"I don't believe my mother would let me," she faltered. "You . . . come with me, and I'll ask her."

"All right," said Earl with a tug at his sled rope.

He waited with his load in front of Maud's house until she came forth, radiant, lugging a big basket. She had her last winter's red cashmere dress, a hood, some mittens, cake, biscuits, and nice slices of cold meat.

"Mother said these would be much more *suitable* for her," said Maud, with a funny little imitation of her mother's manner.

Over across the street, another girl stood at the gate, waiting for news.

"Have they found her?" she cried. "Where are you going with all those things?"

Somehow, Earl's generous romantic impulse spread like an epidemic. This little girl soon came flying out with her contribution; then there were more—quite a little procession filed finally down the road to Jenny Brown's house.

The terrible possibilities of the case never occurred to them. The idea never entered their heads that little, innocent, trustful Jenny might never come home to see that Christmas tree which they set up in her poor home. Thus it was with no surprise whatever that they saw, about noon, Mr. Munroe's sleigh, containing Jenny and her mother and Mrs. Munroe, drive up to the door.

Afterward, they heard how a woodcutter had found Jenny crying over on the east side of the mountain at sunset and had taken her home with him. He lived five miles from the village and was an old man, not able to walk so far that night to tell them of her safety. His wife had been very good to the child. About eleven o'clock some of the searchers had met the old man plodding along the mountain road with the news.

They did not stop for this now. They shouted to Jenny to "come in, quick!" They pulled her with soft violence into the room where they had been at work. Then the child stood with her hands clasped, staring at the Christmas tree. All too far away had she been searching for it. The Christmas tree grew not on the wild mountainside in the lonely woods, but at home, close to warm, loving hearts. And that was where she found it.

Something for Aunt Jane

Elizabeth Flint Wade

Aunt Jane—how near impossible to find something practical that she'd like! Every Christmas it was like this for the four girls.

But this Christmas, they shamelessly dumped the responsibility on Betty, their youngest sister, and Uncle Otis.

* * * * *

The four Avery sisters sat on the floor in front of the sitting-room grate, each with her Christmas shopping list ready for inspection and approval, for Christmas was close at hand.

"Betty," said Adelaide, the eldest of the four, "you are youngest, so read your list first."

"Such a time as I've had making it!" said fifteen-year-old Betty, unfolding a sheet of pink paper. Betty affected pink in everything. "Christmas money doesn't go very far when the thing you want costs twice what you can afford to give. Mine's mostly handkerchiefs, I think."

Betty read her list, which was, as she said, mostly handkerchiefs. It ended with "a handkerchief for Cousin Maria, and something for Aunt Jane."

A shout of laughter went up from the listeners.

"Oh, it's so funny," cried Clara. "That's what my list ends with!"

"Mine too!" said Janet and Adelaide together, and then they laughed harder than before.

"Well, it's nothing to laugh about," said the aggrieved Betty. "I've thought and thought about Aunt Jane—"

"Yes, we all know that, but—"

A loud ring of the bell, followed by the sound of a hearty voice, caused Janet to leave her sentence unfinished, and the four to spring to their feet, rush into the hall, and embrace a stout gentleman who was taking off his overcoat.

"Oh, it's Uncle Otis! It's Uncle Otis!" they cried, seizing him by the hands and pulling him into the sitting room and seating him in a big chair before the fire.

"Yes, it's your Uncle Otis," said the newcomer, "and he's on his way to New York and stopped off to take one of you girls with him. Whose turn is it this time, and where's your mother?"

"Oh, it's my turn, it's mine!" cried Betty, dancing up and down. "Just think of going to New York at Christmastime!"

"Yes, yes, but what about school, little miss?" asked Uncle Otis.

"Oh, Adelaide!" implored Betty, turning to her sister. "Don't you think Mother'll let me skip school if I study all vacation? Do ask her, and you ask her too, dear Uncle Otis!"

The "asking" was evidently effectual, for the next morning the sisters were at the station bidding goodbye to Betty and Uncle Otis.

"Now remember," said Janet, giving Betty a parting hug, "be sure you get something for each of us to give Aunt Jane—and remember it must be useful too."

* * * * *

I'm almost sorry we entrusted Betty with the buying of something for Aunt Jane," said Adelaide as they watched the

45

train disappear in the distance. "She's too young to have good judgment."

"Oh, well," said Clara, "Uncle Otis will help her, and anyway, I'm glad to have it off my mind. I've thought about Aunt Jane's present till my brains are numb."

"Aunt Jane," was the great-aunt of the Avery girls. She lived alone in a small saltbox house on the outskirts of the town. The inside of the house was as unattractive as the outside, and Aunt Jane seemed to fit her surroundings. She wore her hair combed smoothly over her ears and knotted tightly at the back in the fashion of fifty years ago.

The Averys were Aunt Jane's only relatives and would have been glad to have her make her home with them, but she preferred to live in her own little house on her meager income and be, as she expressed it, "beholden to nobody." She would not even accept presents which could not repay in equal value, and the girls found it harder each year to give Aunt Jane something useful and inexpensive of which she did not possess duplicates. No one ever thought of giving anything purely ornamental to Aunt Jane. She sniffed at "foolish furbelows" and apparently cared not at all for the frivolous things of life.

At the time of year when the rest of the world was hurrying to and fro searching for Christmas gifts, Aunt Jane sat by her window and knitted. One year she would knit for each of her grand-nieces a pair of gray leggings, and the next year each of them would receive a pair of knitted red "wristlets." This year was "legging year."

* * * * *

It was a very happy Betty who descended from the train at Bennington a week later. Her sisters were there to meet her and to have a word with Uncle Otis, who could not stop over as he wished to spend the holiday in his own home.

"I'm just brimming over with curiosity to know what you've bought for Aunt Jane," said Janet, when, after supper, Betty, the center of interest in the home group, was eagerly telling the story of her outing.

"Let me show what's in this box first, before I tell," answered Betty, beginning to untie a package. Its fragrance penetrated even the paper wrapper.

She opened the box and took from it a large square of creamy silk so filmy that it floated in the air as she shook it out and tossed it into her mother's lap. To her father she handed a square box of shining lacquer decorated in quaint and artistic fashion. Then she took from the package a small pasteboard box covered with strange characters, and opening it, disclosed a bird of shining metal and a bunch of green leaves and a bunch of flowers which she placed on the table. Last of all she drew from its many wrappings what looked like a jumble of beads and glass and tinted paper. She held it aloft by a string, and it disclosed itself as a hoop covered with beads from which depended long slender strips of glass painted with graceful flowers. In the center was a hollow crystal ball with red fishes depicted on it, looking as if they were alive and swimming in a tiny globe. A long bead of glass with a rose-colored streamer attached was strung through the globe and when the streamer waved to and fro, it caused the bead to tinkle against the globe. As Betty moved the hoop all the glass clashed together, making a pleasing musical sound.

"Oh, Betty, Betty," cried Janet, "where did you get that darling thing and what is it for? Do tell us about it."

"It's a Japanese wind bell," said Betty. "You hang it in the window, and when the wind blows, the glasses jingle and tinkle and make such soft pretty sounds—and this little bird is an incense burner. See, you take one of these leaves or one of the flowers, put it in the bird's bill, set it burning, and it scents the whole room. That box Papa is holding is Japanese lacquer, and the picture on top is of Fujiyama, the sacred mountain of Japan, and the flowers on the sides are Japanese plum blossoms. The scarf on Mother's lap is Japanese crepe, and this"—dipping into the box once more—"is a spray of Japanese cherry blossoms. Don't they look as if they are real?" And Betty waved aloft in pride and admiration a beautiful branch of what looked like real pink flowers.

"Oh, they're the dearest things I ever saw!" said Adelaide, "but, Betty, why didn't you wait till tomorrow? We never have our presents till Christmas morning, and—"

"They're not your presents at all," said Betty. "They're for Aunt Jane."

"*For Aunt Jane?* Why Betty Avery, what made you? She'll never—"

"Tut-tut, Adelaide," said Mr. Avery, seeing Betty's lip quiver. "Tell us about it, Betty."

"Why, 'twas this way," said Betty, standing with her back against the table and speaking rapidly. "We left Aunt Jane's things till the last day, and then Uncle Otis had a telegram to see about some more business, and he couldn't go with me. So he took me to a wonderful store where they had things such as you read about in *Arabian Nights*. He left me in the charge of a girl just about my age, and she showed me the most beautiful things—why they just took my breath away almost, they were so lovely. And I made up my mind I'd get something for Aunt Jane in this very store, and it could be useful, too, and these things are. You know Aunt Jane hangs strips of paper in the window in the summer to keep the flies out, and she can use the wind bell, and it'll scare them twice as well. And she always thinks the hall is musty and burns coffee for it. Now she can burn a leaf or flower. Her handkerchief box is pasteboard and broken, and that lacquer box is wood and will last her years to keep handkerchiefs in. And I thought these cherry blossoms would be nice to put on her Jerusalem cherry tree when its blossoms were gone. And the silk, well you know we think she looks like the picture of Great-grandmother Barnett, and she likes to have us say so, I'm sure. If she would turn in her black silk dress waist in a V and fold this silk handkerchief inside it like Grandmother's picture, she'd look almost exactly like her. I want you all to like the things. I'm sure they're just as useful as they can be," and the tears which had been glistening in Betty's eyes brimmed over, and she hid her face on her father's shoulder.

"Never you mind, Betty, child," said her father, putting his arm around her. "These presents shall go to Aunt Jane, and you girls go now and write the notes to put with them, and I'll take them out to her right away, along with Mother's preserves and pickles. And by the way, perhaps you better explain what each is for."

* * * * *

"I hate to go in, don't you?" said Clara, as next morning the four girls walked up the path to Aunt Jane's door.

"Yes, I do," answered Adelaide, "but let's get it over with. The sooner an aching tooth is out the quicker the pain stops." But before Adelaide could give her announcing rap, the door was opened by Aunt Jane.

"Come right in! It's a proper cold morning, an' go right in my bedroom an' take off your things, an' then come an' git warm."

The girls had time for only a hasty glance as they passed through the sitting room into the bedroom, but that had sufficed to show them a bird on the table with a leaf in its mouth, the glasses of a wind bell glistening in the window, and a lacquer box on a stand, and beside it a pile of neatly folded handkerchiefs.

Adelaide pointed to a chair in the bedroom, and there was Aunt Jane's black silk waist and over it lay the shimmering square of Japanese crepe.

When the girls went into the sitting room, Aunt Jane was on her knees before the stove stirring the fire.

"My, such surprisin' Christmas presents I never had in all my born days!" she said brusquely, giving the fire an extra poke.

"Did . . . didn't you like them?" began Betty, timidly.

"Well, I don't s'pose I'd ought, but I do," said Aunt Jane, still poking at the fire. "I spose livin' as I do from hand to mouth as you might say, I'd oughtn't to even want anything pretty, lettin' alone havin' it, but now I've got 'em, I might as well tell you I've just hankered for some o' the pretty things you girls have, an' I just hated—fer I might as well own up to the whole thing—I've hated the holders an' aperns an' dusters an' dish towels. Why, I've got enough to last me twice as long as I shall live. Look here," and rising, Aunt Jane opened the lower drawer to her highboy, disclosing to the astonished gaze of her nieces, the drawer packed with dusters, holders, and wiping towels, the accumulation of many Christmases of "useful things."

"Look at them holders, I couldn't never use 'em up. Two lasts me a year, an' I've had a dozen every year since I've lived alone, but thanks be, I ain't got a blessed holder this year. And you go get your presents; they're on the table in the best room."

Four small packages lay side by side on the table, and as they looked at them, Adelaide whispered, "It's wristlets, I can tell by the size. She forgot 'twas 'legging year.' "

"I'm going to put mine right on then," said Betty, breaking the string of the package, but instead of wristlets out fell a handkerchief with a lacy border; and the others hastening to undo theirs found that each package held a pretty, dainty gift of the same kind!

"Oh, oh, Aunt Jane!" exclaimed Adelaide, "Wherever did you find these lovely handkerchiefs?"

"Made 'em," answered Aunt Jane, stooping to pick from the carpet a thread that was invisible.

"*Made* them? But you surely didn't make the borders!"

"Oh, yes, I did. It's tattin' made out of number hundred thread, that's what makes it so fine. Last summer I was lookin' over an old box an' found my tattin' shuttle. I thought I'd forgot how to use it, but I hadn't, and then I decided I'd tat 'stead o' knittin' this Christmas."

"But, Aunt Jane, I've seen you knitting every time I've been here."

Aunt Jane had hitherto made no pretense of hiding her Christmas work.

"Well, I thought I'd surprise you for once—and here I'm the one that's surprised. Jes' look at them flowers! They look as if they was growin'. Talk about makin' the desert blossom like the rose! I'll tell you there's folks that has lives like the desert, an' nobody ever thinks o' so much as plantin' a dandelion in 'em, let alone a rosebush. But I ain't goin' to talk 'bout my desert. If one o' you'll pin that handkerchief on my dress, I'll wear it up to dinner this evening, an' you might tell your mother that I'll bring along a change, an' if she wants me to, I think I may stay with you till after New Year's over."

Santa Sylvia

T. Morris Longstreth

Sylvia was beautiful—and knew it. She had a rich uncle who treated her like a princess. She felt like one and loved being treated like one.

So when her uncle invited her to go with him to remote Lunkinville because of the illness of his longtime housekeeper, and travel by sleigh in the bitter cold and snow, she was more than annoyed.

She wouldn't go. After all, Christmas Eve came tomorrow.

* * * * *

Sylvia raised her lovely face, which was slightly flushed from her intense interest in her book, and frowned charmingly. It was not her pleasure to be interrupted just then. Her Uncle Lee stood before her.

"I've received word that my old housekeeper is ill. It's my duty to go over to Lunkinville and see her. I wonder if you'd like the adventure of riding over with me, Sylvia?"

"How soon should we be back?" she pondered.

"Not till tomorrow night."

"Tomorrow night! Why, that is Christmas Eve, and we've so much to do here!"

"I know. And it's a cold ride, and you'd be in uncomfortable quarters tonight, more than likely. On the other hand, I have to go, for Mrs. Hearn was a kind soul, and I cannot neglect her, even for the Princess Sylvia's Christmas, and I thought it might cheer her to have a womanly smile. I also know it would cheer me to have you go. But I didn't invite you up here to be a martyr and still less to expose you to our Vermont blasts on a twenty-mile sleigh ride. What say, Sylvia?"

The girl struggled in her mind, matching her desire to remain by the great hearth and read, with Lee Stewart's subtle compliments. Sylvia was not only old enough to be joyously beautiful, but to be a bit vain, also—spoiled, one could say— and even somewhat selfish. She liked to be called Princess Sylvia, because she knew that she was a Cinderella. Wealthy Uncle Lee was a sort of beneficent prince regent, who gave her things that her own family could not afford and who always invited her to Skyline House for Christmas. In her heart, she knew that she should go with him. But she did not want to leave her luxury and spend the time with poor people; she heard and knew enough about them at home.

"I don't believe you want to come," he said disappointedly.

"Lunkinville sounds so queer and horrible," she replied.

"It is, it is. I wish I could wipe out the huts and poverty there, give the place a new name and a new start, and make all the Lunkinvillers happy. There aren't so many of them. Well, be a good girl and amuse yourself till I get back."

"I'm going," she said, the genuine Sylvia getting the better of the selfish princess. She snapped her book too emphatically.

Lee Stewart brightened. "Really? You're a peach, princess. Put on your knickers [knee-length trousers], then, Sylvia. You'll be warmer. And be ready in half an hour, if you can. I'm going to see that the things are being packed in the sleigh properly."

He left her. She stared into the wood fire. "Oh bother!" was her only comment. *David Balfour* had closed and fallen. She gave the book a little kick with her pretty foot, and then

ran upstairs to dress. A look in her mirror made her smile, however. She had extremely beautiful chestnut hair, darker eyes, a Cupid's-bow mouth, and disappearing dimples. She admired herself. Others admired her beauty. When her inner self should be as admirable as her outside beauty, Sylvia Stewart might well look into her mirror with satisfaction. Perhaps this thought came into her mind, for she put on her knickers and an extra pair of wool socks rather thoughtfully.

* * * * *

"Sure I'll go, Aunt Jen; I'd like it, *sure!*"

Larry Hearn poured some clear tea from a pot on the stove and brought it to the woman propped up in bed with a shawl about her.

"You're a good boy, Larry. Can you remember all o' them?"

"I'm writing them down," said Larry. "Can you think of anything else besides what I've got?"

"We ought to get some Christmas things, Larry. How much money's in that drawer?" Mrs. Hearn sighed so that her nephew should not hear. This poverty, these ills of age, the dreams unrealized for her nephew, the cold—all lashed the memory and the spirit of the woman into a fit of mournfulness, yet she tried to keep cheerful for Larry's sake.

"Seven dollars and thirty cents," announced the boy.

"Then don't get the cod liver oil, dear. I don't really need it, and we must get something for Mrs. Flanders. And then there's Nellie Brown's children; we must—"

"You must get well, Aunt Jen," and the boy, sitting down by her on the bed, looked into her eyes with his troubled eyes of brown, rubbed her wrists with strong hands, adding, "that's what I'm going to bring—wellness for you. And I'll go cut wood for Nellie Brown, and we'll think up something for Mrs. Flanders. And what's more, I'm going to get a job. It's going to be a mighty poor Christmas, but the last poor one, Aunt Jen, for I'm not going to school any longer. I'm near seventeen and—"

"And it's you I depend on, dear."

"Sure! So that's why I quit school."

"But it's school that's making you a great man, Larry. When you come home and read me from that R. L. Stevens man—"

"Stevenson, Aunty."

"Well, Stevenson then—it makes me think of Skyline and the good old days with Mr. Stewart."

"Why don't you write Mr. Stewart?" asked Larry, who had heard of the good old days all his life, but had never tasted them.

"Would you have me begging, boy?" She drew her shawl tight.

"No, but if he's as great and fine and rich as you always say, he'd want to . . . to show you a good time till you get well."

Larry had put on the sweater that his aunt had knit for him in less rheumatic days. He was tall, had strong shoulders, and a face sombered by early cares, but a face which was handsome enough when Larry smiled, a face which cared for reading and for outdoors, a face ever in search of a smile. But smiles were scarce in little Lunkinville that autumn of too early frost, of too severe a famine. Lunkinvillers were used to famine. Old Lunkin, the pioneer who had settled first in that high and beautiful, but unproductive, valley, had died of it.

Larry got his skis from the side porch, saying, "Here's Mrs. Flanders now, Aunt Jen, so you won't be lonely."

"Have you got your lunch?"

"Yep, and don't worry if I'm not back till late. There's a moon."

"Take care of yourself on those awful skis, Larry."

He kissed her goodbye, and she murmured again, "You're a good boy, Larry."

He laughed, "That's the only thing I want on my gravestone," put some more wood in the stove, and left her. Ahead of him was the twelve-mile cross-country ski to Eveson, the nearest place for medicines; behind him, many high hopes. His ambition must have come from his grandparents, for his father had died in debt. He longed to see the world, to tread those streets of Edinburgh where his worshiped Stevenson had walked, to hunt the island of *Robinson Crusoe*, even to see New York. Instead, he must secure his aunt and himself against starvation, against freezing, and get what reading was possible on the side. He halted just outside the door. The road ran down to the little river and disappeared up the opposite slope into a wide view of wooded hills. Everything sparkled under a sun that shone, but did not heat. He buttoned his outer coat, tipped his skis, and went shooting down the declivity, taking the slight turn at the bottom neatly, and flying across the bridge. He noted how black the water was between the floes of ice—swift water, stern ice, and then he climbed and looked back on his tiny village, almost hidden in firs and birches. Despite its poverty, its smallness, its hideous name, it was his home, and he thought it beautiful. He swung along hour after hour. At the same time, Lee Stewart and Sylvia, their breath freezing on their fur coats, were being drawn gaily toward Lunkinville by David and Jonathan, two of the best from the Skyline stables. And Sylvia's eyes sparkled as she took turns with her uncle in driving.

* * * * *

I t's to be a bitter night," said Mrs. Flanders.
"So it is that," said Mrs. Hearn, "and my boy not home yet."

"Well, I must be going."

"And I too," added little Mrs. Dowley. "It'll be a hard winter. I wish I could give the children a nice Christmas. It's hard when you have children, Mrs. Hearn."

"And don't I know, even if he is only my neffy? He's so good to me! And to think he's never known a Christmas like what I had year after year over at Skyline."

"I don't see why you ever left," said Mrs. Flanders, quite truthfully, for she had never been told. Mrs. Hearn offered no explanation now either, contenting herself with a luxurious sigh.

"Is there anything I can do before I go, Jennie?" asked Mrs. Dowley.

"If you'll just poke some more wood in the fire. I wish you didn't have to climb that long hill."

Mrs. Dowley wished so too, for her home was high above the river. She lifted the stovelid, and kept it lifted, listening. "Sleigh bells?" she inquired of the others. "Who'd be driving with bells at this hour?"

"Who indeed?" asked Mrs. Flanders, peering from the window. "Why, Jennie, they look like they was coming here, and society folk." And she made a quick pretense of getting ready to go, without any intention of leaving. There was a knock.

"Will you open and see?" asked Mrs. Hearn, breathing quickly. "I declare, I can't imagine who it is." But her heart stood still, propped high by hope, and then it jumped, once, as she saw the kindly, smiling face of her former employer and heard his hearty voice saying, "Now I've found you! Now you are in for it, Mrs. Jennie Hearn! You wretched, modest, naughty, proud woman!" And his voice, while it uttered these unkind words, was so full of real joy at seeing her that her eyes filled with happiness. This was a meeting she had desired, but had not dared to bring about; she glowed also with pride that her two friends should be witnesses of it.

"And how did you find—"

"How? By the birds and the postmasters and the most expensive kinds of ways," he said, laughing. "And here I am forgetting everybody else in the world. I want you to meet the Princess Sylvia Stewart, my niece."

"And she certainly looks it," said Mrs. Hearn, in turn presenting Mrs. Flanders and Mrs. Dowley, both in a great flutter. Sylvia's heart had sunk at seeing the poor room, these old ladies, the drabness and humbleness when there should have been Christmas preparation and hilarity. She was glad of the plum puddings and the Egyptian shawl and the other gifts in the hold of the sleigh.

"I must be going," said Mrs. Dowley for the seventh time.

"Do you have far to go?" asked Sylvia.

"Just up the hill a piece," said Mrs. Dowley, desiring, but afraid, to intimate how far. Mr. Stewart caught on. "I know what that means," he said, "a mile at the shortest, and we have two horses shivering to be off. I'll drive you, if you can wait till we have got a few things out."

"Oh, but you have driven so far!" said Mrs. Dowley beseechingly.

"I'm going to drive, anyway," said Sylvia. "I was going to suggest it."

"Do you mind returning alone?" asked her uncle, thinking it well that she should plunge into usefulness at once.

"Of course not," said Sylvia; and with Mrs. Dowley still protesting that she was causing a world of trouble, Sylvia tucked her in. As soon as the sleigh was unloaded, off they went down the hill, across the bridge, and up the far side. And she looked down at the black water, feeling its sullen way beneath the stern white floes.

"No, I have never met him," said Sylvia, in response to Mrs. Dowley's effort at making conversation.

"Well, he's a right fine boy, is Larry, though a bit too fond of his books to do the best for himself."

"He is?" said the girl, clucking to the horses, as the hill was steep. "I don't think you *can* be too fond of books, Mrs. Dowley."

"Well, Larry—" and the talk centered around him the rest of the trip. Nor was this strange.

* * * * *

Sylvia was returning. The lights of Lunkinville, all seven of them, shone from across the narrow valley. It was cold, and the horses felt its steel in their blood. It acted like spurs.

"Quiet there, David. Whoa, Jonathan," said Sylvia, as she approached the brow of the hill, "those shadows won't hurt you." A row of firs, broken only by another road entering, threw their gloom across the way. Sylvia shivered. She felt lonely. She wished she were back at Skyline, with its lights and hearth fires and curtains and silver and gaiety. "Steady, Jonathan!"

Both horses had pricked up their ears and stopped. Now they reared back as a gray figure on skis swooped down from the side road, the snow flying behind him. Then, spurred by surprise, by the dark violence of that darting figure, falling like an eagle from the night, they bolted. "Steady, Jonathan! Stop, David!" cried Sylvia, but as well call to antelopes, to shooting stars, to pause a while. The sleigh was nothing; the weight of Sylvia on the reins was nothing; the fear of that griffin behind them was everything. They pulled; they broke into a run; they topped the brow of the hill and started that long descent to the dark river bottom. And Sylvia, bracing her feet in the swaying sleigh, half closing her eyes against

the spray of snow which their flying hoofs kicked up, felt herself being whirled downward, sucked downward into the cold black void. Only vaguely did she wonder whether they would make the curve, whether the sleigh would upset. Now it dashed into the deeper snow on one side, but never quite toppled—the speed was too great. She could not open her eyes, for lumps of snow assailed her. She could not think; the speed, the icy air, the icier fear choked her thought. There was a sort of splendor in such blurring speed, and for one foolish moment she laughed aloud, because the thought that she was Santa behind his reindeer came to her. She could not call to the horses. And now they were approaching the curve before the bridge.

Larry had paused. The horses, the sleigh, were as much a surprise to him as he to them. Then he saw the girl's plight, heard the increasing tumult of her pair, heard her voice breaking in her effort to still them, saw the sleigh dropping downward. Larry visualized the road. He knew they could not make the curve and had an instant's mental view of horses and girl carried out on the river, on the ice, even struggling in the water. Giving himself a mighty push with his ski poles, he was after them. What he would do, he knew not. His speed increased. All afternoon, on his long trudge homeward, he had been counting on this final slide; but never had he thought to have a thrill like this. He was flying now, the purple landscape becoming a mere mist on either side. Ahead he saw the sleigh go over the side of the road, saw it pitch down the riverbank, and he longed to close his eyes. But he kept them open, forced himself not to fall, tempered his great speed in the soft snow of the roadside, and followed the sleigh. He fell, for nobody could have taken that bank in the dark and not have fallen. He picked himself up dazedly, and felt his skis. They were all right. He felt moisture on his cheek—blood. Just a slight cut

from the harder snow, probably. He saw the horses, kicking, rearing in a lather of snow and water. One was prone in the river, the other, in a mortal terror, was demolishing the sleigh with its hoofs. Where was the girl?

A binding, as of an iron band, gripped Larry's throat. The dusk was heavy with cold, the twilight almost impenetrable. He found no trace of her in the sleigh and thanked his Maker in the space of a heartbeat. The horses were slipping into deeper water as they struggled. Flying slush drenched him. He must not stop. He must find her. Was she in that black water? And a chill, more searching than any cold could be, seized him.

Swiftly he started down his side of the river. It widened. Several ice floes were floating. But he saw no girl. He had gone a hundred yards. The river narrowed into dangerous rapids. Below, search was useless. Two floes had grounded. He crossed on them to the other bank and ascended the stream. Suddenly, he felt a branching thrill along his backbone. There was a dark lump on a moving ice floe; yes, there was the girl! But how to reach her, that was the question.

The ice floe was grinding along, slowly, but inevitably, toward the rapids. It was only ten feet from him, but likely to get no nearer. Larry made up his mind. He slipped off his pack, unbuckled his skis, backed off for a run, ran, leaped, landed! He landed with a slide that took him nearly to the other edge of the floe. It dipped; water seeped on and wet the face of Sylvia. She opened her eyes with a shudder, only to see a form bending over her, to feel herself being lifted in strong arms, to hear a deep voice saying, "Are you hurt? Do you hear me?"

She was only half conscious—and heavy. He glanced up in despair. The rapids were nearing! He and his responsibility were getting farther from the home shore. He knew that he must act, even if drastically. "Will you trust me, miss?" he said, and she, hearing the voice of sympathetic strength, murmured, "Yes, what must I do?"

"Put your hands here," he said. "It'll be cold, but we'll make it quick. And don't be scared."

"I won't be," she said, for there was something in his voice that made fright seem something far off.

Grasping him as he ordered, she let herself be pulled into the river. Oh, what bitter chill! She grasped him tightly, as he struck out strongly. Above, the bowl of heaven gleamed with stars; beyond was a ledge of ice, a purple blue. These are all she remembers today, of that terrible, frozen minute.

He held on to her, lifted her, pulled himself up, and they stood, two congealing figures. "We've got to keep going or it's all up," he said. "My aunt's house is at the top of the hill. I reckon you'll be comfortable there."

She laughed nervously, "Are you—Larry?"

"I'm Larry," he said, dragging her into a trot, and she had no breath to say what she wanted, what cried out in her to be said. Those things she stored up for later.

* * * * *

And now later had arrived. In Mrs. Hearn's house, there was a sitting room with a hearth, on the hearth a fire, before the fire a princess with flying, drying hair and stars in her eyes, beside her a shy young man, wrapped, like his companion, in blankets. Lee Stewart stuck his head into the room saying, "Will you children have some more hot lemonade?"

"No, thanks," said Larry, "how are the horses?"

"David is all right; Jonathan's cut leg will come around. The sleigh is matchstick size. But those are minor things. You two can toast just twenty minutes longer, then off you go."

"All right, sir," said Larry to the closing door—and then to Sylvia, "I think you're an awfully good sport to like Lunkinville when we've done such things to you."

"Like pulling me out of the river? Larry, you funny boy, I—"

"Please, Miss Sylvia," and Larry put his hand on hers, "you promised."

"Well," paused the girl, who had promised not to be audibly grateful any more, "I like everything about Lunkinville but the name. I wish it had a name as beautiful as these woods and hills and, yes, even the river."

"I know a name as beautiful as that," said Larry, looking at the stars in the princess's eyes. And he started, his thoughts on an idea.

"What is it?"

"It's . . . it's a—well, it's a secret I have," and he flushed handsomer than ever in the fire glow. "I shouldn't wonder if I'd tell you, though—sometime."

"Now."

"Can't."

"Please. You won't tell me this; you won't tell me what you'd want most for Christmas; I—"

"Oh, yes, if you asked what I wanted most, I'd tell you quick."

"What is it?" and Sylvia prepared to make a mental note of a book list, for she had discovered Larry's craze for reading.

"Well, it's this way, Miss Sylvia. If Santa Claus should come a-driftin' in tomorrow night about this time and say to me, 'Larry Hearn, what'd you like most for Christmas?' I'd shoot him the answer right quick: I'd like to see Lunkinville real happy for once. Nowadays I come in from skiing, feeling smooth as air and contented as those old hills, and then I find Aunt Jen all crisped up with the rheumatics, and Mrs. Flanders stitchin' her eyes out on her kids' stockings, and Mrs. Dowley lookin' peaked 'cause she tries to make her barrel of flour go further 'n a barrel was ever intended to go, and nobody's happy. And that takes it all out of me, and I feel worse 'n the wind in the eaves. Wouldn't you?"

"Yes," said Sylvia, very quietly, thinking of times when she had not been too thoughtful.

"Last call for bed!" cried Lee Stewart, again intruding a smiling face.

"Oh, Uncle Lee! We're having such a good talk," said Sylvia.

"I can only quote Shakespeare, dear. 'Tomorrow and tomorrow and tomorrow.'"

Larry laughed and hugging the blanket about him, rose. "Will you quote some more Shakespeare tomorrow, sir?" he asked. "I'm starved clear to the ribs to hear some."

"Folios of him, Larry. Good night, old man," and the uncle of the rescued princess added a blessing in his handshake. The door closed. "How do you feel?" he asked the princess.

"Never like this before—I'm so happy."

"Funny way to get happy," said her uncle, putting on a blank face, "to throw yourself onto ice floes, swim rivers, and have to be thawed out like a milk bottle. Rather expensive too."

"The expense has scarcely begun," said Sylvia, tweaking his ear. Then, seriously, "Uncle Lee, I want to spend Christmas here."

"What?" And he was surprised. "Leave those presents piled up at Skyline House? Give up the party? Well, I'm delighted, for I was going to suggest the same thing, only I hardly dared, when I remembered the time I had in getting you to come."

"This is what I want to do," she went on. "I want to be Santa Sylvia to Lunkinville."

"You vain thing!"

"Listen," she said, laughing. And, listening, he heard plans that delighted him in many ways. He realized that Sylvia had been awakened to others than herself. He had also found out a good way to begin repaying Larry delicately, and he added suggestions which extended the bounds of Sylvia's idea. When they left for bed a full hour later, it was a certain thing that Lunkinville was in for a Christmas such as it had never known.

* * * * *

It was nearing the middle of the afternoon of Christmas Day, and the feast was over. All Lunkinville had pushed back its chairs from the long table made of boards and set up in the little church, the one building that would hold them all. If Lunkinville could have purred, a most contented noise would have arisen from that assembly of twenty-nine souls. For Lunkinville had seen Santa in the flesh and had breathed of the spirit of happiness. Surprise after surprise had taken its other, and more usual, breath; for such goings to and fro, such preparations, sendings of messengers, impressment of sleighs, such cookings and candy makings and stocking fillings and importation of curious packages had never gone on in Lunkinville.

Sylvia, the star-eyed, had risen the next day none the worse for her accident; and she, with her Uncle Lee, had set Christmas Eve a-rolling. She, with lists, with whisperings and quick consultations, had been the spirit of surprise. Larry had been her right-hand man. Mrs. Hearn had offered much wisdom from her bed—now she reclined like a Roman matron at the foot of the feast table—and Mrs. Dowley's four children had been invaluable messengers. Indeed, when a whole village at once gets working together under the leadership of a merry and wealthy man of affairs, it is pitiable if a good deal of happiness does not result. There was now nothing pitiable about Lunkinville.

And now the Lunkinville children, as stuffed as the turkeys which once had sat before them, and surrounded by gifts, were exhorted to quiet by their parents. There was to be one more surprise, a surprise which they all knew about, and which neither Lee Stewart nor Santa Sylvia knew anything of. Larry, rising, stood, a very modest hero, till the last giggle had subsided. Sylvia thought she'd never seen anybody with so frank and happy a face, with eyes so brown. She wondered

what was going to happen. This was not on the program.

He had begun to speak: "Friends," he said, "I've got to make a speech—'cause nobody else would. But I reckon I can get through with it, for I've got something to say—*two* things, really. One can't be said by me entirely, for it's our thanks to Mr. Stewart. I reckon each of us'll have to say that to him straight. I can only say for myself that he's opened up things and feelings I've never had, just as when I've come to a hilltop and looked out over things new and beautiful. But you can't say thanks to the hill; you can't say thanks to Mr. Stewart well enough. But you can *live* thanks—and he appreciates that kind.

"Then there's the other thing. It's about Miss Stewart, naturally. It was the other night that she and I were talking about this village. Miss Stewart said she thought the woods and hills and even the river, where she'd just had a ducking, were mighty beautiful. She said she wished our village had a name as beautiful as all those things. So did I, and what's more, a name as beautiful as all those things came right into my mind. But I didn't mention it, not till I'd seen all of you, separately, and found out we agreed that the name of Lunkinville had better be put into the grave with good old Mr. Lunkin." The boy, flushed a little, but, still master of himself, turned to Sylvia. "So here, Miss Stewart, is the paper that we've all signed, asking the state to let us change our name. We all feel mighty grateful to you; we all feel something else too. We feel as if we'd like to have you with us always. So, if you don't mind, we ask your permission for the town to be known as—on the maps, that is, and in the geographies and at the post offices—to be forever known as Sylvia, Vermont."

The applause came. It came ahead of time, but so spontaneously that it was better so. Larry waited till there was a lull, then he added, "Will you grant us this final gift, Miss Stewart?"

Her uncle nudged her. Sylvia rose, eyes bright and beautiful.

"I . . . I think this gift that . . . that you are making to me is the most beautiful Christmas present in the world. I thank you more . . . more than I can ever tell—" And since her breath quite failed, she sat down, in an uproar of hand clapping and a circle of smiles.

Larry's deed was done; he began to edge his way toward her.

"Oh, vain one," whispered Sylvia's uncle to her, "are you happy?"

"Not quite," she said, smiling.

"No?" he said, astonished, for Lee Stewart was immensely pleased.

"No," said Sylvia, "for I know I shall never be so happy again," and she held out both hands to Larry, "unless—"

"Oh! That," said Lee Stewart. "That was decided long ago. Larry has agreed to spend the week with us—and longer if he can stand it."

"What a way to put it!" cried the girl, trying to tease. "And now we'll have him running back in no time to—"

"Sylvia," said Larry, with a happy grin.

Baby Deb "P'ays" for the Christmas Goose

John Russell Coryell

It was a bleak Christmas for the lighthouse keeper and his family that year—around 125 years ago. The children could accept the absence of presents, but not of a goose for Christmas dinner. So it was that—secretly—Baby Deb prayed that "Dod" would send them a "doose."

* * * * *

Christmas is just as much Christmas at the Boon Island Lighthouse as it is anywhere else in the world.

And why not?

To be sure, the nearest land is ten miles away; and when the winter storms come, the waves dash quite over the two acres of rocks out of which the sturdy lighthouse rises. There are no blazing rows of streets lined with toy shops there; no gatherings of families; no Christmas trees loaded down with presents; nothing to be seen from the lighthouse but the changing water and the unchangeable rocks. Water on three sides, and on the fourth side a bluff barrier of rocks, with a world hiding behind it ten miles away.

There are six children there, though, and a mother and a fa-

ther. And if they cannot make a Christmas, then nobody can.

Why, Baby Deb alone is material enough with which to make a Christmas, and a very rollicking, jolly sort of Christmas too. But when to her you add Tom and Sue and Sally and Ike and Sam—well, the grim old lighthouse fairly overflows with Christmas every twenty-fifth of December.

If it is a lonely, old, one-eyed lighthouse, has it not a chimney? And do not the children there have stockings—good, long stockings? Indeed, they have. And does not Christmas Eve see them all temptingly hung, so invitingly limp and empty, under the mantelshelf? And does not Christmas morning—very early, mind you!—see six graduated white-robed ghosts performing their mysterious ceremonies around six bulging stockings?

Ah, then, if you suppose that that cunning old gentleman, Santa Claus, does not know how to find a chimney, even when the cold waves are pelting it with frozen spray drops ten miles from land, you little know what a remarkable gift he has in that way!

And the Christmas dinners they have there! The goose—the brown, crisp, juicy, melting roast goose! What would that dinner be without that goose? What, indeed!

But once—they turn pale at that lighthouse now when they think of it—once, they came very near having no goose for Christmas.

It came about in this way: Papa—ah, if you could only hear Baby Deb tell about it! It would be worth the journey. But you cannot, of course, so never mind. Papa Stoughton—the lighthouse keeper, you know—had lost all his money in a savings bank that had failed early that December.

A goose is really not a very expensive fowl, but if one has not the money, of course, one can not buy even a cheap thing. Papa Stoughton could not afford a goose. He said

so—said so before all the family.

Ike says that the silence that fell upon that family then was painful to hear. They looked at one another with eyes so wide open that it's a mercy they could ever shut them again.

"No goose!" at last cried Tom, who was the oldest.

"No goose!" cried the others in chorus. All except Baby Deb, who was busy at the time gently admonishing Sculpin, her most troublesome child, for being so dirty. Baby Deb said, "No doose!" after all the others were quiet.

That made them all laugh. No doubt they thought that, after all, so long as Baby Deb was there, it would be Christmas anyhow, goose or no goose. So they were happy for the moment, until the thought came that roast goose was good on Christmas even with Baby Deb. And then they looked dismayed again.

However, when Papa Stoughton explained how it was, they saw it as plainly as he did, and so they made no complaint. Only Tom fell a-thinking, and when the others saw what he was doing, they did the same; the difference being that Tom was trying to think what could be done to get the goose anyhow, and they were trying to think what he was thinking about, so that they could think the same.

All except Baby Deb, of course, who, being only four years old, gave herself very little concern about the thoughts of others. Her own thoughts took all of her time.

Tom finally said "Ah!" under his breath and mysteriously vanished into another room after beckoning to his brothers and sisters to follow him, which they did almost before they had fairly said "Ah!" Baby Deb was there too; somewhat awestruck at the mystery about her, but ready to lend the help of her wisdom, if necessary.

"We *must* have a goose," said Tom.

"Oh!" gasped his audience, moved by mingled amazement and admiration.

Tom looked at them with great firmness and dignity.

"Ever since I was born," he went on, "we have had a roast goose for Christmas."

Ever since he was born! It might have been a hundred years before, from Tom's tone and manner, and the audience was tremendously impressed.

"And," continued the orator, "we must have one now. We *will* have one now."

They almost stopped breathing.

"I have a plan." They shuddered and drew nearer. "We all must contribute!"

"Oh!" in chorus.

"Do you want a goose, Sue?"

"Yes, indeed."

"You, Sal?"

"Yes."

"Ike?"

"Do I? Well!"

"Sam?"

"Yes, *sir*."

"Me too," said Baby Deb, with great earnestness; for it was clear to her that it was a question of eating, and she did not wish to be left out.

"Of course, you too, you daisy dumpling," said Tom. "Now, then," he continued, when order was restored, "what shall we contribute? I'll give my new sailboat. That ought to bring fifty cents."

His new sailboat! Why, he had only just made it and had not even tried it yet. Oh! Evidently this was a time of sacrifices. Who could hesitate now?

"I'll give my shells," said Sue, heroically.

"My sea mosses," sighed Sally.

"You may take my shark's teeth," said Ike.

"And my whale's tooth," said Sam.

The sacrifice was general; the lighthouse would yield up its treasures.

"All right," said Tom. "Now let's tell Father."

Father was told, and for some reason he pretended to look out of the window very suddenly; but he did not, he wiped his eyes. And Mama Stoughton rubbed her spectacles and winked very hard and said, "Bless their hearts!"

For, you see, these parents were very simplehearted folk, and it seemed to them very affecting that the children should make such sacrifices to procure the goose for Christmas.

"And what does Baby Deb contribute?" said Papa Stoughton, by way of a little joke.

"I dess I's not dot nuffin," was Baby Deb's reply when the matter was explained to her, " 'cept 'oo tate Stulpin."

Oh, what a laugh there was then! For if ever there was a maimed and demoralized doll, it was Sculpin. But Baby Deb was hugged and kissed as if she had contributed a lump of gold instead of a little bundle of rags.

Papa Stoughton and Tom were to go out to the mainland the first clear day to buy the goose; but—alas!—a storm came on, and they were forced to wait for it to go down. It did not go down; it grew worse and worse. The wind shrieked and moaned and wrestled with the lonely tower, and the waves hurled themselves furiously at it and washed over and over the island, and no boat could have lived a moment in such weather.

If a goose be only a goose, no matter; but if it be a Christmas dinner! Ah, then!

Yes, they had good reason to feel dismal in the lighthouse. It was no wonder if five noses were fifty times a day flattened despairingly against the lighthouse windows. Yes, six noses, for even Baby Deb was finally affected; and, though she did not know the least thing about the weather, she, too, would press her little nose against the glass in a most alarming way, as if she thought that pressure was the one effective thing.

It took some time for Baby Deb to realize the importance of having a goose for Christmas, but when she had grasped the idea, she became an enthusiast on the subject. She explained the matter to her dolls and was particularly explicit with Sculpin, with whom, indeed, she held very elaborate and almost painful conversations.

One thing became very certain. There was very little prospect of clear weather within a week, and it lacked only three days of Christmas. The others gloomily gave up hope, but not so did Baby Deb. The truth was, she had a plan; and you know when one has a plan, one has hope too.

Mama Stoughton had only recently been having a series of talks with Baby Deb on the important question of prayer, and it had occurred to Baby Deb that the goose was a good subject for prayer. It was a very clear case to her. The goose was necessary. Why not ask for it then?

The great difficulty was to find a secret place for her devotions, for the family completely filled the lighthouse, and Baby Deb had understood that prayers ought to be quietly and secretly made.

The place was found, however. Just in front of the lighthouse was a broad ledge of rock, generally washed by the waves, but at low tide, even in this bad weather, out of water. The other children had been forbidden to go there because it was dangerous, but no one had thought of cautioning Baby Deb. So there she went and in her imperfect way begged hard for the goose.

Christmas Eve came, and still there was no goose. Baby Deb was puzzled; the others were gloomy. Still Baby Deb would not give up. It would be low tide about seven o'clock. She knew that, for she had asked. She would make her last trial. She had hope yet, but as the others knew nothing of her plans, they had absolutely no hope. To them it was certain that there could be no Christmas goose.

Seven o'clock came, and Baby Deb crept softly from the room and downstairs. She opened the great door just a little bit and slipped out into the darkness. Really did *slip*, for it was very icy on the rocks, and she sat down very hard. However, she was very chubby and did not mind it. She crawled cautiously around to the big rock, the keen wind nipping her round cheeks and pelting her with the frozen drops of spray. She knelt down.

"Oh! Please, dood Lord, send us a doose. We wants a doose awful. Won't you, please, dood Lord?"

Thud! fell something right alongside of her.

"Oh! What's dat?" she exclaimed, putting her hand out. "Why, it's a doose!" she cried, with a scream of delight, as her hand came in contact with a soft, warm, feathery body.

She forgot to give a "thank You" for the goose, but she was thankful, though not so very much surprised. She really had expected it.

It was a heavy load for Baby Deb, but she was excited and did not notice it. She made her way into the lighthouse, and, step by step, patter, patter, she went upstairs and burst, all breathless, into the sitting room, crying exultantly, "It's tummed, it's tummed," as the great goose fell from her arms upon the floor.

Well if you think they were not surprised, you know very little about the Stoughton folks. What they said, nobody knows. They all talked at once. But by and by, Papa Stoughton had a chance to be heard.

"Where did you get it, Baby Deb?" he asked.

"Why, I p'ayed Dod for it!" answered Deb.

"Paid Dodd!" exclaimed Papa Stoughton.

"Paid Dodd?" chorused the family.

" 'Es," responded Baby Deb, convincingly. "Dod—Ze dood Lord. I p'ayed to him. He sended it to me, dess now."

More questions and more of Baby Deb's explanations revealed the whole story. Funny folk, those Stoughtons!—but they spent the next ten minutes wiping their eyes and hugging and kissing and making up new pet names for Baby Deb.

Papa Stoughton did say to Mama Stoughton that night, as they were going to bed, "A wild goose. It was blinded by the bright light and broke its neck by flying against the glass. And, after all, who shall say that 'the good Lord' did not send it?"

At all events, not a word of explanation was said to Baby Deb, and no one contradicted her when she said at dinner next day: "Dod's doose is dood."

A Snowbound Christmas

Frances Cole Burr

It was quiet in the train car, each traveler thinking about Christmas in one way or another. Though they sat so close to each other, they remained total strangers.

Until the train stopped.

* * * * *

Most of the occupants of the small room sat gazing out of the windows into the snow-filled air. There were windows enough to go around, though the room was long and narrow and contained six or eight persons. All day they had spent together in this one room, each sitting quietly in his place. There had been but little conversation. The tall dark man with the white mustache and tired face had slept much, with his head resting on his folded overcoat. A boy opposite, who showed sullen anger and defiance in every line of his young face, had watched him and wondered how a man could sleep in the daytime. The boy did not know that those long, nervous white hands, wielding a surgeon's knife, had saved a life the day before, and the tired eyes had watched for many hours following.

An earnest, bright-faced young girl nearby had observed him too, while he slept, as she eyed all her neighbors with keen interest. There was the old lady in the corner, a man with sample cases piled at his side, the shabby little woman holding a big baby, and a middle-aged man with a stolid, joyless countenance, who had read three newspapers through from beginning to end without a change of expression, and since then had sat staring straight before him. The girl in her active mind had tried to combine these various personages into a story, but she gave it up with a little sigh for their commonplaceness.

An ill-assorted company it was. Surely they would have chosen to spend the day before Christmas together for no other reason than, as it happened, they all wished to travel over this branch road, which ran between the northern line from Little Falls and the Grand Central.

The day was nearly over, and the journey should have been; but the snow, which had been falling steadily since morning, grew heavier; the speed of the train perceptibly decreased, and the engine groaned and labored. The engineer watched apprehensively as they drew near a certain cut, narrow and deep, through the hills. It was drifted high, and meeting that soft, still, resistless opposition, the great engine slowed and stopped.

The drifting snow hid the familiar landmarks, and so it happened that just as the passengers were anxiously questioning one another as to the cause of the stop in that lonely place, Jim Case, the fireman, swinging himself off the engine, slipped over a culvert, and in the fall of only a few feet, broke his arm with startling ease and completeness. He was lifted back, white and fainting; and, when the brisk conductor hurried into the passenger coach, he responded to the anxious queries with a brief "Snowed up," and then, addressing the dark man, he said, "I don't suppose you're a doctor, are you?"

"Yes," said the man, with an inquiring glance. "Does someone need me?"

The conductor looked relieved.

"Now, ain't that luck!" said he. "Surgeon too, I guess?" The doctor nodded assent. In a few words the conductor told of the accident amid exclamations of mingled sympathy and dismay from the listeners. And as the doctor picked up his small black bag and followed him into the forward car, the conductor continued, "Not many of you travel on this road, but I thought that was your trade when I took your ticket. I gave a job to a surgeon once when I was hurt in a wreck. That was a good while ago, but I have never forgot the look or the feel of his hand—so steady and strong," he added with an apologetic smile.

"Here we are, Jim!" he called out cheerily. "Here is the doctor and the head nurse. You just break your bones, and we will do the rest, you know."

The fireman lay stretched upon the floor, his head resting languidly on a pile of waste; a pretty five-year-old boy, sobbing with fright, was kneeling close beside him.

"Who is this little fellow?" asked Dr. Carleton, after the examination was over and he was skillfully bandaging the injured arm.

"He's mine, poor little chap!" said the fireman, with a tender glance, though his lips were white with pain. The boy, who was a sturdy little fellow just out of dresses [in those days both boys and girls used to wear dresses until about four or five years of age], stopped his sobs as he heard his father's voice, and looking up at the doctor asked, "Now will we go to Grandma's and have a Christmas?"

The man winced again and closed his eyes, and the conductor explained in a kindly aside, "Little chap's mother is dead; just buried her a week ago. She had him filled up chock-full of Christmas, and seems as if he couldn't give it up. They are going on to Jim's mother's. She's going to take care of Ja-

mie; and I guess the old lady had promised to have a tree."

Jamie was listening eagerly, and he broke in, forgetting his shyness, "Yes; a Christmas tree and candles. For Grandma said so."

"Seems as if that is all he thinks of," said the fireman. "His poor mother—she—" and he stopped and closed his eyes again.

"Shall we go now?" insisted Jamie. "You said that we'd get there the night before Christmas."

"Now, young fellow," broke in the conductor, "you know this is road luck. You are a railroad man and must learn to keep a stiff upper lip when things go wrong. Brace up, and let that tree wait a day or so."

But Jamie's sobs broke out afresh. Fireman Jim's head turned resignedly away.

"I should think some of those women might know what to do for the boy," said the conductor. The doctor nodded.

"Take him away and have him amused if you can," said he. "He troubles his father. He ought to have something to eat," the doctor hesitated and then added, "though I suppose it does no good to say so. Have you anything—any way of making a cup of tea or any beef extract? Do you go prepared for these emergencies?"

The conductor shook his head. "I'm afraid not," he said, "unless some of the passengers might have something left from lunch. We were due at five thirty, you know, and we get our supper in town."

"Well, you might inquire," said the doctor. "He would feel better after having a bit of something."

So the conductor, carrying the crying Jamie, went back to the passenger car. He found the young girl the center of what seemed almost a social circle.

The good-natured baby, who had been drowsily nodding,

was sound asleep in one of the farthest seats, as content as a veteran traveler in a Pullman stateroom, while his mother sat shyly on the outskirts of the little company. The traveling man's sample cases, covered with a napkin, formed an improvised table, and upon this the stock of eatables was being spread.

"Well, anyhow, we shan't be starved," the old lady said. "That there basket"—pointing to a huge covered wicker—"is full of fixin's I was taking to John's folks. I expect it won't seem so like Christmas to the children if they don't have them leaf cookies and the gingerbread animals, and they are good if I do say it that oughtn't. But I'm sure I never thought, when I was bakin' 'em, that they would save our lives."

"We'll hope they need not do quite so much for us," laughed the pretty girl, whose name on the one modest trunk in the rear car was D. M. Marsh, "but we will not touch the children's cookies unless we are starved into such robbery. How glad I am Aunt Mary made me take this great box of luncheon! I hardly made an impression on it this noon." And she brought out an unopened jar of pressed chicken. "This will be our Christmas turkey!" she announced.

"Isn't there some way of melting that down into soup?" asked the conductor, who came in just at this point.

"How is the injured man?" inquired the commercial traveler, while the old lady held out her motherly arms for Jamie, as she said, "You poor lamb! Is it his pa that's killed?"

"He's all right," said Conductor Brooks, "only his arm is broken, and he is knocked out and faint. The doctor was asking for some soup or something to brace him a little. If that was chicken broth, now, it would just fit."

"Why, we can make broth in just a few minutes," said Miss Marsh, and in a moment she had brought from her trunk a pretty chafing dish and lighted it, the old lady nodding

approval. "Alcohol too," the girl said, laughing, "left over from the last spread at college."

The lamp was quickly adjusted, and into the bright pan went part of the jellied chicken.

"It's a privilege, nowadays, to see a young girl know somethin' about cookin'!" said the old lady, while the stolid-faced man silently proffered a match, and Jamie stopped crying to taste the broth when an appetizing odor began to diffuse through the car.

During all that had passed, the boy had hardly left his dark corner. He did not wish to talk. It was nobody's business where he was going, and someone would be sure to ask. But he looked on and thought how bright and quick and pleasant the girl was. When the broth was sent to Jim, and the doctor returned, the remainder of Aunt Mary's bread and butter and pickles was spread, with various additions from the others' lunch baskets. Part was reserved for breakfast, and the little group whose common misfortune had thawed all reserve supped together merrily, if not bountifully. The boy declined all but a single sandwich. He was hungry, but the angry, defiant pride which had hardened his face all day melted somewhat, and he felt less like eating.

"And tomorrow is Christmas!" said the traveling man, whose name was Osgood. "I've worked like two men to get through and have the day at home with the wife and babies, and it is hard to be stalled up so near."

"And there's my son John and Milly and the children. I haven't missed a Christmas with them since John was married. They all come to me Thanksgivin'," said the old lady, "but we're all alive, and that's a great mercy."

"Never mind," said Miss Marsh, "we'll have the evening at home. But I wish I hadn't stayed with Aunt Mary until the last moment."

"I want a Christmas!" sobbed Jamie, his ready tears bursting forth again. "Mama said I should have a Christmas; an' Gramma's got a tree, an' I–want–a–Christmas!"

Again the big conductor told the short, sad little story of the dead mother who had promised a happy day to the boy; and Miss Marsh looked steadily out of the car window a half minute, while her eyes brightened and a resolve formed.

"Jamie boy," said Miss Marsh, "you shall have your Christmas. It's Christmas here just the same as all over the world; and you shall have a real one."

He looked up in joyful trust. "An' a tree?"

"Yes, dear, a real tree," said the girl. The others listened in astonishment. The old lady opened her lips to remonstrate, but shut them again. The traveling man whistled softly and skeptically, and the doctor looked on amused. Only Jamie and the boy gazed at her with implicit confidence.

"When shall I have it?" asked Jamie.

"Tomorrow—Christmas morning," said the girl brightly. "Now go to Papa and go right to sleep, and in the morning, you'll see!" With tears undried, but with a face beaming with happiness, Jamie let himself be carried away to his makeshift bed by his father's side.

"An' a tree," he said, as the sleepy eyes closed, "an' candles, an'—"

* * * * *

Well?" said Mr. Osgood, with a quizzical smile of doubt. But before Miss Marsh could reply, the boy said briefly, "I'll get it. I saw 'em before it got dark."

He had already buttoned his coat, and seizing the red-handled ax that hung near the stove, he bravely leaped out into the drifts.

"Those little evergreens, you know," said Miss Marsh, "they are just a few feet away. He can see them by the light from the windows, I think. And we can make it pretty somehow," she continued eagerly. "Jamie's such a little lad, and Christmas means so much to him."

Mr. Osgood nodded.

"But what's goin' to be on the tree?" asked the practical old lady. "It's all foolishness goin' to so much trouble for that one child, and we a-tremblin', you may say, between life and death! But I declare for 't, I hate to have the day go by and do nothin'. And even if we're rescued tomorrow, as that conductor says he thinks probable—which I don't more 'n half believe—what with gettin' home, and explainin' when you do get there, which please mercy we may! why, the day's as good as gone. An', anyhow, I've got a pair of red knit mittens for John's Alexander, and I'm going to give 'em to that poor motherless lamb, an' you can hang 'em on the tree for one thing, Miss Marsh."

"Splendid!" said Miss Marsh. "And I have a red skating cap in my satchel. I believe it will just fit him."

"Is he too small for a knife?" asked Mr. Osgood. "Let's see—about five, isn't he? My wife makes six the knife line; I guess I'd better not." And he returned it to his pocket.

"Hold on!" said he, with sudden inspiration. "I've some illustrated catalogues here that could pass for picture books—yes, and cards too—our new ones," and diving into his cases, he brought out a pile of brilliant pictures.

"Will Miss Santa Claus accept this?" asked Dr. Carleton, offering a pocket microscope. Just then the door opened, and the boy came in, dragging triumphantly a small evergreen.

Everyone laughed excitedly, and it "did begin to seem somethin' like," as the old lady said. Then how they worked! The tree was braced firmly at the end of the aisle, the lumps of ice and snow shaken off, and a more durable quality of soft cotton flakes from Dr. Carleton's surgical stores added. Leaf cookies and astonishing gingerbread animals dangled from the branches, and Alexander's red mittens waved in welcome. Even the man of the immovable visage helped, with something like a softening of his hard features. And when he fastened to a branch a red blank book and pocket pencil, there was an outburst of laughing applause.

Meanwhile Dr. Carleton talked quietly with the shabby little woman; he asked about the baby's teething, and she unconsciously gave him much of her simple story. Her husband had lost his position in the little town where they had lived. He had found work in the city, and she was going to meet him. They had no "folks." She'd worked in a factory before she was married. No, the baby hadn't cut any teeth yet. She hoped she wouldn't fuss or be sick about it. She didn't know much about babies. The doctor listened with sympathy, and, a little later, wrapping a bright gold piece in a bit of paper, he marked it, "For Baby Burns to cut her teeth on," and it was added to the tree.

The boy looked on with a dull ache in his throat. He hoped it was not going to be sore. How sick he had been with those bad throats, and how good Mother always was! Mother was filling the children's stockings at home now. She always managed to have something for them, somehow. Poor Mother! She would have it all to bear alone now. How could he leave her? Why hadn't he thought of her part? *But I won't go back,* he said to himself. *I can't go back now. I'll come home rich some day and give Mother everything she wants. But I won't sneak back now.* Then he didn't care to think more.

"I can make a top," he whispered to Miss Marsh, "if I have a piece of wood. Shall I?"

"He would like it best of all, I know," said Miss Marsh

heartily, and then she added, "now we must have a star for the top. What can we do about it?"

"Well, I guess it's good enough," said the old lady. "I guess he won't miss the star."

But the girl looked from one to another in perplexed appeal.

"Why must there be a star?" asked the boy shyly.

Miss Marsh hesitated a moment. She did not know much about boys, this brotherless college girl, but she said, almost as shyly as he, "Don't you think the Christmas star is the most beautiful thing in the world? You know the Christ child was born beneath a star, and I think it meant, for one thing, that for every new life there is a star set in heaven that will light the life all the way, if once we catch a glimpse of it and know it is there for us."

The boy listened breathless. He could not have told just what the girl's words meant, but the moral courage that all day had been struggling to live took new strength and slowly began to shape itself into a resolution. They stood looking at each other, when the traveling man, who was down again in his cases, emerged in triumph, waving some tinfoil.

"Cut out the star from that pasteboard box," he cried, "and here's the glory for it. We can't stop short of perfection in this tree."

"Well, I'm blessed!" said Conductor Brooks, staring at the sight, when he came in a little later. "Where do you folks think you are? At a Sunday School festival?"

"Never you mind where we be!" said the old lady. Her bonnet was awry, and her spectacles on her forehead. "You just help h'ist up that star, and then we're all done."

* * * * *

Christmas morning, Jamie woke round eyed and expectant.

"I want my tree," he said, "and I want my breakfast." And as the waiting holiday makers were impatient as he, the breakfast was hurried through, and then they all filed in—Jamie in Conductor Brooks's arms, his father, who was doing bravely, coming behind, followed by the engineer. Jamie gazed at the tree as if dazed by his surprise, but after the first moment, a smile of radiant, ecstatic joy spread over the round, babyish face. Not a word or sound—only that beaming, blissful smile. It was irresistible, and with shouts of laughter the tree was despoiled of its offerings, and Jamie's cup of happiness was full. In the midst of the merriment Miss Marsh

glanced at the boy. He was gazing at the star with a curious expression, and she thought of their words the night before. In her bodice was thrust a pin whose head was a tiny golden star—the badge of her class society. She drew it out, and pressing it into one of the leaf cookies which were being passed about, she handed it to him with a whispered "Merry Christmas!" He saw it, and there was a quick rush of color to his face and tears to his eyes—and that little star weighed down the balance of decision on the right side and made a man of him. But the girl never knew.

When the laughing talk had quieted a little, Jamie turned confidently to Miss Marsh. "Now the story," he said.

"What story, laddie?" she asked.

"The Christmas story. Mama said there is a Christmas story, and she saved it up for Christmas Day. It is 'the nicest story I ever heard,' Mama said."

Every one was still for a moment. Poor Jim turned away. *She would have made a good man of him,* was the thought in his heart. The girl felt her own heart beat quickly. Could she? Before all these strange people? What would they think! No, she couldn't; she would have a chance to talk to Jamie alone before the day was over. That would be much better. But the childish eyes gazed expectantly into hers, and with a swift thought of the dead mother, she lifted the little boy gently to her knee, and with softly flushing cheeks and voice that trembled a little, she began, "Long ago, in a beautiful country over the sea, there were shepherds in the fields keeping watch over their flocks by night."

The sweet voice grew stronger as the simple words of the wonderful story held the listeners in solemn silence. The little woman's tears dropped on her baby's head as she heard of the mother for whom there was no room in the inn, and a vague, trembling prayer went up from her burdened heart to the Christ who was a child.

The boy's eyes shone with new light as he thought of the star set in heaven for the Christ who was a boy, and with a thrill of newly awakened love and appreciation he placed his own weary, hard-worked mother on her throne in her boy's heart.

There were eloquent sermons preached in the churches that Christmas Day, and wonderful music was sung. But, as truly as in his visible temples, Christ was preached and worshiped about that little tree, whose balsam breath went up as frankincense and myrrh.

* * * * *

A little later in the day, after the relief engine had come and the train pulled into the city station, the Christmas party stopped a moment for the last handshakings and farewells. Twenty-four hours before, they would have parted with scarcely a glance at one another. Now they seemed old friends. The busy doctor hurried away first, followed by a long, grateful look from the baby's mother.

I'll never forget it of him, she thought.

The boy took a step toward Miss Marsh. One of her hands was tight in Jamie's chubby clasp; the other was held in the old lady's.

He looked a moment, then turned with a resolute face, and walked to the ticket office.

"Give me a ticket on the first train that goes back to Little Falls," he said.

Hetty's Letter

Katharine Kameron

Eight-year-old Hetty Williams was an orphan; in fact, it appeared that nobody in all the world cared whether she lived or died—except perhaps for Miss Thankful White, but even she did not realize how starved the little girl was for love.

Or for a wax doll.

* * * * *

This story is 120 years old.

* * * * *

Miss Thankful White's "keeping room" was as prim and proper as herself. Hetty Williams glanced about her, as she knitted briskly. Long practice had made this easy for her. The chairs stood stiff and straight against the wall in rows. The ancient sofa held itself severely erect, while its long lines of shining nail heads made her arms ache to look at them. She had polished their bright brass every day of her life, as far back as she could remember. The square-figured carpet was spotless, even the feathery asparagus that filled the fireplace never dropped a grain. The great pink-lined shells on the high chimney shelf, and the scraggy coral branch, had stood in the same places always, and the tall bunch of peacock's feathers, with their gorgeous colors and round eyes, nodding over the whole, were worst of all. "They stare so," she said softly under her breath. The dismal green curtains were down, to keep the

sun from fading the carpet, but the summer wind fanned them in and out and brought to Hetty bright flashes of goldenrod along the roadside and the sweet scent of the buckwheat and the drone of the bees above its white blossoms. The door to the kitchen was closed. Miss Thankful had a visitor and was enjoying a good gossip.

"Take your knittin', Hetty, and run into the keepin' room, and shut the door after you," were Miss Thankful's instructions when Widow Basset had seated herself comfortably in the flag-bottomed rocker. The session was longer than usual, and Hetty grew desperate.

"Miss Thankful," said she, clicking the latch and putting her small head into the kitchen, "may I take my knittin' out under the big tree in the orchard?"

"I'd jest as lief as not," was the answer, "if only you don't get to dreamin' and forget your work. The mittens must be done afore Sat'day night, you know."

For a while the needles flashed in and out, the mitten grew longer, and the work went on steadily and quietly, as if Hetty had been one of the newly patented knitting machines. The sunshine made shadow pictures on the grass, the leaves over her head rustled pleasantly, and the leaves at her feet waved silently in a tangle of light and shade. The bees went humming by, and the butterflies brushed her face, but still the little maid worked faithfully at her task. The last mitten was nearly finished.

Suddenly the sound of chattering voices and merry laughing caused her to look up in surprise. Three little girls were coming toward her, and one of them said, quite politely, "We saw you here and thought it looked like such a nice shady place for our dolls' picnic. Would you mind if we stayed with you to play?"

"I should be very glad, indeed," answered Hetty heartily,

but she scarcely looked at her little visitors—her eyes were fixed on the dolls which two of them carried. Hetty had a ragdoll of her own making, hidden away in a box under her bed, and it was one of her most precious possessions. She had seen prettier ones at the store and had long dreamed of saving pennies to buy one—but these dolls! These were so unlike anything she had ever seen or imagined that they "took away her breath," she said. They had dainty wax faces, with cheeks like rose leaves, and great blue eyes with dark, silky lashes, and real golden hair, wavy and long. *They must be meant for dolls' angels*, Hetty thought, but said not a word. She was not given to speaking her mind, Miss Thankful White's motto being: "Little girls must be seen, but not heard."

While she stood lost in admiring wonder, the little strangers, with a busy chatter, set about preparing their picnic. Before long, Hetty knew that they lived in Boston and that they, with their mama, were boarding at the Maplewood Farm, nearby for the summer; that two of them were sisters, and one a cousin. All this, and much more, was told to their new neighbor.

Presently Hetty said thoughtfully, "I guess little girls are heard in Boston."

They looked at her a minute in surprise, and then one answered, "Why, yes, of course; aren't they in Patchook?"

"Miss Thankful says they should only be seen," was the reply.

"Who is Miss Thankful?"

"Why, she's Miss Thankful White, and I live with her."

"Is she your aunt?"

"No. She's the one who took me to bring up, when Mother died—to help 'round and save her steps and do the house chores." Hetty made this long speech quite rapidly, as if she had heard it, or said it, so often that she knew it by heart, and then she fell to knitting busily.

Her little playmates looked at her and at one another, but did not answer. This was a kind of life they knew nothing about. They could not imagine a little girl without a papa and mama, auntie and cousins, plenty of toys and playtime, and lots of laughing and talking.

Soon one of them, with a bright thought, said quickly, "Would you like to hold my dolly, while I help set the table?"

This was delightful. Hetty dropped her mitten and taking the dainty creature gently in her arms, she lightly smoothed the long, soft dress of finest frills and laces. What a wonder of beauty! Hetty sat silent and happy, stroking the golden hair and touching the little hands and pretty kid shoes.

"Where did it come from?" she asked at length.

"Uncle Charley bought it for me at one of the Boston shops," answered the little owner, carelessly. A wax doll was nothing special to her.

Then Hetty took up the other doll and compared them— *a brown-eyed beauty, and a blue-eyed angel,* she thought.

Suddenly she heard Miss Thankful's voice calling, "Hetty! Hetty Williams! Can't you see it's near sundown? How are the cows to get home if you don't spry up and start after 'em?"

Sure enough, the day was nearly done, and when the little strangers started for Maplewood Farm, long, spindling shadows, with long, spindling dolls in their arms, ran alongside of them. Hetty saw this, as she stopped to look back after them on her way to the house.

Then off she trudged after Sukey and Jenny, but she passed by the flaming goldenrod, the purple asters, and the creamy buckwheat without ever once seeing them. It was like walking in her sleep. Her eyes were open, but she saw nothing except the pretty doll faces she was dreaming about.

After the cows were home and the milk in the bright

pans, she finished the last mitten and bound it off in the fading light. Before she slipped into her little bed, she took her dear old ragdoll from the box for one look.

It was dreadful. She shut her eyes tight and put it back quickly out of sight. Those lovely doll angels! She could not quite keep them out of her prayers, even. It took a long, long time for Hetty to go to sleep that night. Her restless head tossed from side to side. When, at last it lay quite still, and she was fast asleep, it was still full of rosy dreams. Blue-eyed dollies, with pink faces and wavy hair, crowded about her pillow.

The first beams of the morning sunshine found Hetty standing in the middle of the floor, with a brand-new idea caught tight and fast in her tangle of hair. Miss Thankful had not called her. She was not even stirring yet, and Hetty spoke aloud, "Miss Thankful will take the mittens to the store today—that makes six pair—and Mr. Dobbins will send them to Boston. That is where the doll came from."

In a minute more Hetty had found a pencil and some scraps of paper and was seated by the low window, busily writing. It was clearly something very important. She wrote one note and tore it up, and then another and did the same; the third time it seemed to suit her. Next, she folded it very small and flat. Then she took the new mittens from the drawer and tucked the folded paper close up into the tip of the right hand.

* * * * *

"Good morning, Miss Thankful," said Mr. Dobbins. "Want to trade fur mittens agin, do ye? Well, that little girl o' yourn makes 'em 'mazin' spruce. None o' the knittin' machines beat Hetty much. We kin get rid o' all ye kin fetch. A Boston man was in here yist'day and spoke fur a dozen pair. So help yerself, Miss Thankful; got some extra fine cotton cloth, very cheap, and some hansum caliker as ever you see."

Hetty was at the south door as the old chaise drove up and took the parcels from Miss Thankful. She saw the mittens had not come back. "Gone to Boston," she whispered joyfully, as she turned into the house again.

So they had—started that very day. They did not stay long in Boston, however. The city was full of western merchants, buying for the fall and winter. Among the rest, stacks of woolen gloves and mittens went off over the iron tracks, up into the great, cold northwestern country, where Jack Frost has jolly times playing his Russian pranks, and nipping noses, ears, and fingers.

* * * * *

Time went by, and winter came in dead earnest. Jack Frost enjoyed his rough jokes and found his way through all kinds of mittens. The clerks of a great store up in Minnesota were tired of saying to customers, "We are out of woolen mittens, sir—all gone long ago—not a woolen mitten left in the house, sir."

"Hello, Mike, what is this?" said a pleasant-faced young fellow to one of the porters, as he drew out a packing box from a dark corner in the cellar.

"Shure an' I dun' no, sir. I'm thinkin' it's sumthin' that's hid itself away, unbeknownst loike."

"We'll find out quickly," said the young man. Mike's hatchet went splintering and cracking through the dry wood till the cover flew off.

"Wullun mittens! Misther Tom, and tis the lucky find, sir. Shure the paaple'll be twice gladder to have thim now, sir, than in the warrum wayther whin they come, sir."

Tom laughed at Mike's sharp way of dodging the blame and ordered them brought upstairs to be put on the counter at once. As he turned away, he took up the top pair. "First come, first served," he said. "These are my share. My old ones leak the cold everywhere." Sitting down by the glowing stove, he examined his prize at his leisure. "Good, thick, warm wool," said he. "No thin places; honest work, first quality."

By this time, two or three others had gathered around him, each with a pair of the new "find." When Tom tried the fit of his new mittens, his fingers touched something in the very tip of the right hand. Turning it wrong-side out, he found a carefully folded paper, like a note. Smoothing it out on his knee, he read it aloud:

My name is Hetty Williams. I am eight years old. I live in Patchook, Mass. I knit these mittens for Mr. Dobbins's store. I wish the gentleman who buys them would send me a wax doll. I have only a ragdoll, and I want one with a wax face and blue eyes and pink cheeks and real hair. I want her very much indeed.

"Hurrah for little Hetty!" said Mr. Tom. "She shall have her wax baby for Christmas Day." And then he fell into a brown study. The fact was, Tom had been born "away Down East," and he had worked a while in a country store there. He knew in a minute just what Mr. Dobbins's store was like. He fairly smelt the soap and fish and coffee, and could see the calicoes and dishes and woolen socks and gray mittens. It did not take long to think through all this, and then he cried, "Who wants to help get a stunning doll for little Hetty? I'm glad Mr. Dobbins sent her mittens along this way."

The boys who did not get notes in their mittens tried to think that Hetty had knitted them all the same, and when Tom passed around his hat, the halves and quarters rattled in. Then a silver dollar thumped down, and a greenback or two fluttered in silently. Tom took the proceeds and went to the busiest toy shop in town and found a famous wax dolly. It was as big and as plump as a live baby and much prettier, he thought. It had a long white frock and shut its eyes properly when Tom laid it down to count out the money to pay for it. It did not take long to pack it snugly in a smooth box. Then Tom pasted Hetty's open letter on the cover. He went down himself with it to the express and told the boys it must go free and that everyone might send a Merry Christmas to little Hetty till the lid was full of good wishes. I doubt if there ever was so much writing outside of one box. Every man who handled it seemed to think at once of some little sister or daughter or niece, and for her sake sent a greeting to the little girl in Patchook.

* * * * *

The day before Christmas, Miss Thankful White's old chaise stopped at Mr. Dobbins's store and post office, and that lady, with Hetty to carry the parcels, came up to the counter.

"Good mornin', Miss Thankful—wish ye Merry Christmas—fine frosty weather, this. Le' me see: I think there's a letter for your little gal, Hetty there—came this mornin'. Get it out, Dan."

Hetty's eyes opened wider than ever before in her life. A letter for *her*! What could it mean? Mr. Dobbins must have made a mistake. But no, the red-haired boy, Dan, read the address, and handed it straight to her.

"Miss Hetty Williams, Patchook, Mass."

Her first letter! She never thought of opening it—she was too much astonished and too excited.

"Sakes alive! Hetty Williams, what be you standin' there for, like as if you was struck dumb? Why don't ye hev sense enough left to open that letter and find out su'thin' about it?"

But as Hetty did not stir, Miss Thankful took it from her hand, removed her glasses, wiped them and put them on again, then carefully opened it and slowly read aloud: "There is a box for Hetty Williams in the express office at Fitchtown. Will be kept till called for. This express does not deliver in Patchook."

"Wall, to be sure! Who kin it be from? How kin we git it?" queried that lady helplessly.

"Why, bless ye, Miss Thankful, that's as easy as rollin' off a log. My boy Dan is jest hitchin' up to go to Fitchtown express for some store goods. He'll bring Hetty's box along with him, and glad to."

Just after early nightfall that day, Mr. Dobbins's wagon rattled up to Miss Thankful's south door. Miss Thankful and Hetty both rushed out to meet Dan, and it would be hard to say which was the spryer of the two.

Miss Thankful took the box from Dan with many thanks and carried it into the house, saying, "It's rather big and hefty for you, Hetty." And then the good woman carefully pried off the cover with a claw hammer and stove lifter. The Christmas softness had, somehow, found its way into her heart, and so she quietly moved away to put up the "tools," and left Hetty to unfold the wrappings by herself and first see the sight, whatever it might be.

Hetty, when Miss Thankful came back, sat as still as a statue, with folded hands, looking only at her treasure. Miss Thankful settled her spectacles, took one good look, and then exclaimed, "Wall, I never! This does beat all natur'. Where upon airth did it ever rain down from?"

Just then, her "specs" grew dim, and the old lady took them off and wiped them well. Then she continued, "Deary me, deary me! Well, I am right down glad that the Lord's put it into someun's heart to clap to and send that child a doll baby. I'm sure I never should 'a' thought o' such a thing, if I'd lived a thousand year, and yet how powerful happy the little creetur' is over it, to be sure! She looks like a pictur', kneelin' there by the box, with her eyes shinin' so bright and so still, just as if the doll baby was an angel, come down in its long white frock."

I only wish Tom could have seen Hetty then, or afterward, when she sat by the bright wood fire, looking with childish delight into the soft blue eyes of her wax darling. Or if he could have taken one look at the two heads on the pillow of the little attic bed that night—both pairs of eyes fast shut and Hetty's small arm hugging her treasure tight and fast in her soundest sleep—he would then have known to a certainty that little Hetty Williams was to have at least one happy Christmas.

A Substitute for Mildred

Helen M. Girvan

The entire Grey household revolved around Mildred and her very well-trained voice. But tonight Mildred had more important things to do than sing for the Christmas program for hospital children. Almost flippantly, Mildred agreed her sister Jane, untrained though she was, could substitute.

Jane was filled with terror.

* * * * *

Thump! The rapid fingers of the girl at the piano slowed at the sound. There it was again—*thump, thump!* This time the fingers quivered to a stop, while Jane tilted a wistful glance at the ceiling. That would be Billy, her small nephew, pretending that he was Galloping Ginger. Ever since he had been taken to a moving picture of a horse race, Billy had delighted himself, if not the rest of the family, by galloping about in imitation of the favorite, whose name he could not even pronounce, and there was still enough of a child in Jane to envy him.

But when only silence greeted her listening attitude, the young girl turned somewhat wearily back to her practice. For perhaps half an hour she worked over runs, trills, and chords until a difficult passage was completely mastered. Suddenly she relaxed, her arms dropped to her sides, and her gaze wandered to the window. Preoccupied with her music, she had failed to notice the first lazy flakes, and now she looked out on Philadelphia through a swirling mass of snow.

A white Christmas! Jane's heart sang at the thought. Half laughing, half solemn, she shook a resolute little blonde head at the piano. "No more today—not another scale!" she told it, waving an airy hand to the instrument before she turned and ran upstairs.

In the room above, where her mother and Jane's married sister Florence Dowling, were sewing, Jane was greeted by a shout of joy from Galloping Ginger, alias Billy Dowling, who immediately tackled her about the knees and demanded, "Thing, Aunt Jane! Thing 'bout the pussytat." Billy lisped just enough to make him seem even more adorable than he really was.

"Pussycats, indeed!" objected his young aunt in high disdain, rushing him excitedly to the window. "Snow! Look at it, Billy. Sleigh rides and snow fights, all the things you've never even seen before!"

"Jingle bells, jingle bells, jingle all the way," she sang gleefully, dancing about the room, a wholly charmed Billy close at her heels.

"Have you finished your practice for the day, Jane?" questioned Mrs. Grey, looking a little anxiously at her youngest daughter.

Jane's wistful eyes pleaded for her. "Don't you know that it's Christmas Eve, Mother, and it's snowing? How can I possibly put my mind to it?"

"Of course not!" chimed in her sister. "For goodness' sake, let her have a holiday, Mother. She can exercise her voice singing to Billy," Florence added, laughing. "He never gets enough."

Jane had little Billy on her lap now and rocked as she

sang, "Over the river and far away." But her face lit up as her mother acquiesced, "Very well; only I hope you have those accompaniments in shape to play for Mildred?"

Jane nodded. She didn't interrupt Billy's song to mention that it was Mildred's accompaniments and not her own singing exercises that she had been practicing so conscientiously.

"And oh, what fun it is to ride in a one-horse open sleigh!" she ended joyously.

"Thing it again!" ordered Billy.

But for once his order was not obeyed. From the doorway a tall, imperious-looking girl issued a rapid fire of orders in her turn. Mildred's height, together with her reddish gold hair and amber-colored eyes, gave her a striking appearance. She managed to make Florence look bedraggled, and Jane, for all her slender youth, a little faded and washed out. Even Billy was silenced. Somehow, when his Aunt Mildred was about, the center of the stage ceased to be occupied by his important young self. Wherefore Billy cherished a secret dislike of her. He could not be prevailed upon to utter a word when Mildred was present.

"Quick, everybody!" called the girl in the doorway, "I've got to be ready in less than an hour. Pack my bag, Mother, while I bathe and change. Florence, if you'll just mend that violet chiffon evening gown where it has come untacked; and Jane, get my music together and come up while I dress, and I'll tell you just what I want to take. If there is time, I would like to run over one or two things.

"Hurry, all of you. I'm leaving on the three o'clock train for New York. Mrs. Merwin, the rich one, is having a last-minute dinner party this evening, and I've been engaged to sing. It's a splendid opportunity. But I have a luncheon engagement downtown and a lesson to give before the train leaves, so we haven't a minute to waste."

Mrs. Grey had started up in nervous reaction to her daughter's hurried commands, and Jane hastily put Billy off her lap and got up to go in search of the music. Only Florence spoke: "I thought you were supposed to sing at the children's hospital, Mildred, at the Christmas party they are giving them this afternoon. How did you get out of that?"

"Oh, my goodness!" Mildred's tone was impatient. "I forgot entirely about it. Well, I couldn't have sung, anyway. I cannot neglect an opportunity like this, for charity. We need the money I'll make—or I do, for those singing lessons I've arranged to take from Blanchard."

Florence shrugged her shoulders, bestowing upon the speaker a rather scornful little smile before she bent over her sewing. But Mrs. Grey drew her brows together in a disturbed frown. "It seems unfortunate, Mildred," she protested mildly. "Mrs. Peabody, who asked you to sing at the children's hospital, has been very helpful to you. It seems a pity to disappoint her."

"Well, it can't be helped, Mother. She must understand that I have my bread and butter to consider. Call up the hospital, Jane, and explain that I've been called to New York and cannot sing. And then hurry upstairs."

"It seems to me," remarked Florence dryly, "that the very least you can do is to call up the hospital yourself and offer to send a substitute."

Eagerly Mrs. Grey upheld her. "Yes, Mildred. I do think, for your own future good, if nothing else, you ought not to irritate Mrs. Peabody."

With one hand rumpling Billy's hair, Jane had been standing watching her sister, some of the child's own awe reflected in her eyes. But it was not awe of Mildred. She was thinking of the children's party at the hospital and the disappointment of the little tots when the entertainment provided for them

failed to materialize. Sympathetic and imaginative, she could visualize their disappointment, because she knew how Billy would feel if she refused to sing to him. And more than that, she knew how she herself had felt, not so very long ago, either, when she had been so sick and fretful getting over the measles—the time when Mildred, despite her plaintive coaxing, had been too busy to sing to her.

With the remembrance partially shutting out their conversation, Jane heard her mother's voice and Mildred's only faintly. Then she heard Florence insist, "Of course, you can send a substitute, Mildred. You can send Jane."

At the mention of her own name, she looked up in alarm. "Send me? To sing? What are you talking about, Florence? Why, I've never sung in public—you know that. There isn't enough of my voice, anyway."

But Mildred interposed with crisp decision. "That's not a bad idea, Florence. It will smooth down Mrs. Peabody, and the children won't know the difference. I'll call up and explain while the rest of you get started. Now hustle, everybody. We've no time to lose."

For the next hour everybody obediently rushed. The hospital having agreed, if somewhat ungraciously, to accept Miss Jane Grey, there was nothing left for Jane to do but submit. The music was found, the violet chiffon mended and packed, and at one o'clock Mildred was off, calling back as she picked her way down the snowy steps to the waiting taxi, "Oh, by the way, Jane, they wanted me to wear something white at that hospital party, so you'd better." Then she was gone, leaving three relieved people behind her.

But Jane turned a look of blank dismay on her mother and sister. "Mother, I haven't anything white. The only thing was that old dotted swiss, and it went to pieces the last time it was washed. What shall I do?"

"Really," Florence's voice had a sharp edge, "it seems to me the only person in this house who *does* have any clothes is Mildred herself. However," starting up the stairs, "that being the case, she probably has something white."

"But we mustn't touch anything of Mildred's!" protested Mrs. Grey, while Jane repeated automatically "of Mildred's."

Florence, however, was already on her way to Mildred's room on the top floor. She came down almost immediately with something white over her arm. "Here's the very thing—that white crepe she had last summer that shrunk so badly when it was cleaned. I don't know why she hasn't given it to you long ago, Jane. She cannot wear it herself, for it's too small." Florence held up the dress. "It's as good as new and simple enough to suit you."

"But do you think we ought—" began Mrs. Grey.

"Of course, we ought!" interrupted Florence. "We are going to, anyway. This is a case of necessity. It's just a little summery looking for Christmastime, though. If only—" she paused thoughtfully. Then her face lighted up. "I've just the thing!" she announced. "And it won't take me half an hour to go around to the house and get it. Meanwhile, Mother, get Jane a cup of tea and make her lie down for an hour. Do you realize that she is going to sing at four o'clock, and it is after one now?"

Jane relaxed in utter content after she had something to eat and a cup of tea. She couldn't go to sleep, but she lay there thinking how pleasant it was to be waited on and fussed over, understanding for the first time why Mildred demanded so much attention. Doubtless, in the beginning it had been showered upon her, until now she had come to insist upon it as her due.

It was a novel but delicious feeling. A princess, Jane supposed vaguely, even a poor princess, would always have someone to wait on her. It would have been rather nice if she had been born a princess, instead of just Jane Grey. Still, princesses, along with their ability to conjure serving maids out of the blue sky, were a little out of date. If she were a prima donna, as Mildred was going to be, it would answer the same purpose. The idea of a family with two prima donnas in it made Jane's lips twitch with amusement, even supposing her voice should turn out to be anything later on. To imagine what it might be like, however, was very pleasant. Silken garments, scented baths, and all the rest of it—furs in winter, gossamer gowns in summer, a home in the country for her mother, and at least a dozen dogs. It drew itself out into such a rambling, but delightful, little daydream that Jane started up almost as though she had been asleep when Billy poked his curious head around the door. He had been sent to awaken her.

"Why, it's almost three," she protested stupidly when she had followed him into her mother's room, "and I haven't practiced a song!"

"And you are not going to. Look!" Florence held up the white dress on which she and Mrs. Grey had been sewing.

Jane gasped. Bands of soft, snowy-white marabou around the bottom of the skirt and edging the neck and the short sleeves made the simple summer frock into a picture dress—just the thing for a Christmas party!

"Oh! It's exquisite!" The girl who was to wear it laid a reverent hand on the soft, downy marabou. "But," as she remembered, "I am going to sing. I will have to go over some of those songs Mildred gave me to practice."

Florence laughed at her, "You must array yourself in this furry frock, my dear, and go to the hospital. You are not even going to take any music."

Jane was bewildered, "But I don't understand."

"Well," Florence informed her, "Mother and I think you

would be crazy to try any of those things Mildred has given you. Nothing so ambitious will be expected of you. Just sing the things you know without the notes, the songs Billy teases for again and again—the Christmas song you were humming this morning, that sort of thing."

"Oh, do you think that would be all right?" Jane was doubtful. "I wouldn't mind singing those things; I'd love to. Would they be satisfied with them though?"

"They will have to be satisfied," Florence spoke emphatically. "Now don't even think of what you are going to sing until you get there."

It sounded a feasible and wonderful plan until Jane found herself actually inside the children's hospital brushing off the snow and removing the various wraps and things that had been pressed into service to protect her from the weather. When she finally stood clear of them, in the white marabou frock and the little white kid slippers that Florence had lent her, she looked almost a child herself. So much so, that the nurse who led her upstairs was openly curious. Presently she opened a door and stood aside to let Jane pass in.

For a moment the young girl stood there uncertainly in the shadowy corner that had been screened off for the entertainers; but almost at once a woman in a rather large hat came up to her, while Jane, immediately in awe of this haughty personage, explained shyly who she was.

"I see." The amazed stare which took Jane in from head to foot contradicted the words. "And I am Mrs. Peabody." She spoke with cold impatience as she added, "It was very upsetting for your sister to disappoint us in this way at the last minute. I cannot understand it."

Whereupon, the comfortable and feasible plan seemed suddenly ridiculous. Jane began a nervous apology, ending up by saying, "I will do the very best I can, Mrs. Peabody. Per-haps the children will not mind—that is, I mean, notice—as older people would." She reddened with embarrassment as she corrected herself. It was quite evident that Mrs. Peabody was much annoyed. Moreover, her attitude said plainly that she had no confidence whatever in Mildred's substitute. Jane repeated helplessly, "I'll do the best I can."

"Of course, you will, my dear. Of course, you will," assented the older woman, thawing a little. "But you are scarcely more than a child yourself. However," as her keen eyes seemed to fathom Jane's growing nervousness, "I am certain of one thing, and that is that the children will love to look at you." She eyed the marabou dress with distinct approval.

As Jane tried to smile her thanks at this encouragement, a feeble attempt, Mrs. Peabody swung about briskly, "Now, listen to me a minute, all of you."

Everyone looked up—the small, foreign-looking man who was occupied in arranging a table with various colored silk pieces and balls and tumblers, the pretty woman in the fur toque, and the nurse who stood beside her.

"Under the circumstances," said Mrs. Peabody, "I am going to announce a slight change in the program. I'll put Signor Fillani first, and Miss Sawyer can give her recitations next, instead of having Miss Grey sing. We will have the songs last, just before we have the tree and the gifts. Now that is understood, isn't it?"

They all assented, Jane nodding in dumb misery. Mrs. Peabody seemed to be doing her best to make it hard for her. She hadn't actually said it in so many words, but her idea was very plain. If Jane's singing was not a success, it could easily be stopped in favor of the Christmas tree and the gifts. Moreover, Jane realized that in listening to the others she would have time to get even more nervous. She had never heard of Signor Fillani, the sleight of hand performer; but at the mention of Ruth

Sawyer, she caught her breath, for Miss Sawyer was perhaps the best-known monologist in the country.

Now Jane had played Mildred's accompaniments often enough to scorn people who let themselves be a prey to stage fright, but she could not help feeling that this was different, because it was something she, personally, would never have been asked to do. She was only there on sufferance because Mildred had failed them. And Mrs. Peabody had managed to make the sufferance part so plain! The thought sapped any remnant of confidence she had left. As Signor Fillani went out in front, she realized that she was trembling.

Just then Miss Sawyer beckoned to her to come over and watch the children through the crack in the screen, and Jane caught her first glimpse of her audience. The big ward was full. All the children who were well enough to stand the excitement had been wheeled in, cots and all, while all the convalescents, together with several visiting children, were arranged facing the great Christmas tree, beside which stood a small grand piano. Farther back, beyond the children, were a number of women interested in the hospital, as many nurses as could be spared from other duties, and a few of the doctors.

But it was the children who caught Jane's interest, especially the little dimpled girl in the front row, with round, roguish blue eyes and hair that clung in short, tight curls close to her head. One tiny arm was bandaged, but she had apparently forgotten it. Her dimples quiet, her eyes wide, she followed every motion of Signor Fillani. Next to her was a boy slightly older than Billy, with his head swathed in bandages and his homely little face thrust forward in a desperate attempt to catch the rabbit in the very act of getting into the hat—else how could he possibly come out?

"If someone should quietly remove the roof and allow it to snow right into the ward, I do believe he would be perfectly oblivious to the fact," whispered Miss Sawyer, smiling.

Jane nodded. "Look!" she whispered back. "That little dimpled rogue beside him is asking Signor Fillani why he can't bring a kitten instead of a rabbit out of the hat—a white kitten. Oh!" she added in a hushed whisper, "It is wonderful to keep them absorbed like that."

The older woman glanced at her. "You mustn't worry," she spoke reassuringly, "youngsters love music above everything else."

Later, Jane almost forgot her own coming share in the performance while she listened to Ruth Sawyer. She caught herself clapping, there behind the screen, as excitedly as the children did when that talented woman had finished one of her recitations. So it came to her with a fearful suddenness, when Miss Sawyer stepped back, that now it was her turn; she was going to sing.

Then she was out in front, being formally introduced by Mrs. Peabody. "And your music, Miss Grey?" questioned that lady in an anxious aside. Jane was speechless. Oh, why hadn't she brought something! She simply couldn't think of anything to sing. All those expectant little faces turned toward her. It was terrifying. She couldn't disappoint them!

In that dreadful moment her eyes met the twinkling blue ones of the baby girl just below her. Whereupon the little child reached out a chubby hand to stroke the marabou on the bottom of Jane's dress, and murmured, dimpling shyly, "White pussy!"

Jane smiled thankfully back—she could have squeezed the darling—and was able to answer Mrs. Peabody in a confident undertone, "I haven't any music. I'm just going to sing to the children." She sat down and struck the first note. Her cue had been given to her.

"The Owl and the Pussy Cat went to sea
In a beautiful pea green boat."

sang Jane, straight at the little dimpled girl at her feet.

Afterward she sang a lullaby that Billy always teased for and the "Birthday Song," because she had loved it as a child herself and the old-fashioned Christmas song that made the boy with the bandaged head sway in time to the jingling bells. The children drank in the music hungrily, and the nurses, doctors, and hospital patrons were forgotten. Jane might have been singing to Billy himself as she caroled tenderly, her eyes on the star at the top of the Christmas tree, " O Little Town of Bethlehem. "

She couldn't know that back near the door sat a man with a ruddy face and almost white hair who was leaning forward to catch every note. Nor could she know that one of the children in the cots was his own boy, nor that he was a director in the hospital. But his name, had it been mentioned, was one that she knew very well indeed, that often and often she had heard.

Jane sang the message of hope and peace with no thought save for the children, and, as she finished, a nurse furtively wiped her eyes, the solemn little lad in the front row blinked and swallowed, while the white-haired man at the back winked away a curious mist that had come into his eyes and started a frantic search through his pockets for his spectacles.

Jane only saw that her childish audience was altogether too solemn, and immediately she broke into a rollicking little nursery song, full of trills and laughs that made them fairly gurgle with delight.

Meanwhile, the man at the back finally located his glasses and his program and found the name. *Grey?*—that was familiar—*Mildred Grey*. That was it. *Couldn't be this little girl, though.*

For a moment he watched the children, all who were able to, crowding around the piano and clapping and stamping. Then he sought out Mrs. Peabody. "Who is that girl?" he demanded. And when she had explained, "Tell her . . . no, don't tell her anything. Where does she live?"

But Jane didn't hear any of this. She was the center of a group of clamoring children, for all who were able to do so, had crowded about the piano, beseeching, "Sing it again— sing more." "More!" echoed a feeble voice from one of the cots.

Jane wished she could sing on forever and satisfy their hungry little hearts. But there was the tree and the gifts. Mrs. Peabody reminded them of that and restored order, smiling a grateful smile at Jane. "Thank you, my dear," she said kindly. "You have given us all a great deal of pleasure."

She seemed to mean it. It was not that, however, which made Jane stay to watch the children with their Christmas tree, so conscious of a warm throbbing joy through her whole being. It was the knowledge that she had been able to give so much pleasure to those children simply by singing the simple songs that she hummed at home all day. Did music affect older people that way, she wondered, if one had a really good voice, as Mildred had?

Later, Jane was strapping on her galoshes when Miss Sawyer in her long fur coat paused before her. "Can't I take you home?" she asked cordially. "I have a car outside, and I think it is still snowing."

Jane hesitated. It was hard to refuse, yet . . . "You see," she explained, "it so seldom snows at Christmas in Philadelphia that I can scarcely remember when it has before. If you don't mind, I think I'll walk." Her cheeks were flushed as she confessed, "I like to feel the snow, to realize it; it seems to bring the Christmas feeling so much closer." She did not add that

she wanted most of all to hug to herself the glow that had come to her when the children enjoyed her singing.

Ruth Sawyer nodded her understanding. "My dear," she said softly, "there is not the slightest doubt in the minds of any of us who heard you sing but that you have the Christmas spirit, and quite enough of it to spare."

Only a few belated flakes were falling, but it was a white, snow-clad world that Jane ventured out into—a world of scurrying, package-laden figures, of friendly lights from windows whose owners had neglected to draw the blinds, and of fascinating glimpses through some of those same windows, of trees to be trimmed, crackling fires, and children dancing up and down with excitement and anticipation. Jane trudged along, enjoying every step and thinking that it was a pity to have to go out of this snow-enchanted world. But remembering that they had planned to go over to Florence's in the evening to help trim the tree for Billy, and knowing also that her mother would be waiting in keen anxiety to hear how she had filled Mildred's place, she quickened her steps.

"It came out all right, Mother," Jane hastened to reassure her the minute she was inside the door. "I doubt if anybody but Mrs. Peabody had ever heard Mildred, so they couldn't know what they missed, and the children were satisfied. Oh, Mother, they were such darlings!"

Just as she spoke, the doorbell clanged sharply, and Jane pulled off the last of her snowy things and hastened to answer it. "Maybe it's Santa Claus himself." She laughed excitedly. "This is just the kind of a night old Santa would love."

The laughing words died abruptly on her lips, for the little man upon whom she opened the door, with his ruddy face and white hair, might easily have impersonated the genial old gentleman she had just been speaking of.

Jane stood gazing at him, speechless. "I see I am not mistaken in my understanding that Miss Grey lives here," he hastened to say. Then, "May I come in?" he added as Jane continued to stare. "It's a pretty bad night outside. Nice, though!" he chuckled. "Reminiscent of old times." He had stepped inside and closed the door behind him before Jane found her voice.

"My name is Blanchard, Walter Blanchard," said the man, calmly proceeding to remove his coat.

At which Jane's gasp was echoed by her mother, for in a musical household such as theirs, the name Blanchard was as familiar as it was highly honored. They heard it several times a day from Mildred herself.

Mrs. Grey at once stepped forward. "And you wanted to see my daughter. I am so sorry that she has gone to New York for the night." She led the way into the plain little living room as she spoke, and Jane and their visitor followed.

Mr. Blanchard spoke gruffly. "I understand your daughter was scheduled to sing at the hospital this afternoon. I can only say I am glad she didn't. Other reasons aside, it gave me the pleasure of hearing this young lady," he turned to Jane and bowed, "a pleasure for which I wish to thank you, my dear."

Jane was gazing at him in astonishment. "But . . . but Mr. Blanchard, I didn't know I—" she stammered in utter confusion.

Mrs. Grey hastened to enlighten him. "My youngest daughter does not claim to be a singer. She has had but little training, and she was merely trying to fill in for her sister. She has had some training as a pianist, but—"

The little man waved an arresting hand. "Yes, yes, I know. I quite understand. It is your older daughter who is the singer. This little girl hasn't much of a voice, and the money has all been spent cultivating her sister's voice."

Jane and her mother exchanged a look. His insight was a bit uncanny.

"Sit down, both of you," he ordered gravely. "I have something to say to you. Although it is not generally known, I happen to be a director in the children's hospital. Now it is just one of the places of its kind which depends on the charity of people like Miss Mildred for such an entertainment as we had this afternoon. And people like your daughter feel entitled to break their engagements at the very last minute if they care to. I consider it a mistake to have to ask such people to sing for charity, especially when children enter in, but often it is that or nothing.

"As I listened to your songs," he nodded at Jane, "a plan I have long had in mind took on a more definite form. Happily, I know enough influential people to make it possible. Briefly, it is this: I would like to take some girl who has the right kind of a voice and train her to sing for just such occasions as the party we gave the children today. Out of the fund we would create, she would be paid and paid well, but she would always be at our command, whether it was to sing to one sick child or for a great number of people hungry for music. She could have no other career—she would have no time for it."

He checked himself abruptly.

"What do you think of it?" he demanded.

Jane's shining eyes and rapt face showed what she thought of it, but Mrs. Grey's expression was a mixture of gratitude and uncertainty. "And you are going to offer my daughter this opportunity?" she marveled. "It seems to me a wonderful thing, but," doubtfully, "I wonder whether Mildred—"

"Mildred? Ah," the little man shook his head impatiently, "my dear Mrs. Grey, I wouldn't dream of offering your daughter Mildred this opportunity. She wouldn't consider it one, to begin with; but aside from that, her voice, well trained as it is, lacks precisely the quality I want.

"A quality," he turned to Jane, "of which this little girl possesses a rich store. Some people, a very few, have in their voice a certain sympathetic quality that reaches the heart. If in addition to it they have the range and quality of tone, a great singer is made. Unfortunately, the combination is rare." He paused.

"I do not think you have the range, my child. It is a pity. However, it is not necessary for the plan I speak of. What do you think of it?" he asked, addressing himself directly to the young girl.

A dozen questions and answers crowded to Jane's lips, but they were all hushed by one thought. She voiced it in an awed tone, "Why, you really *are* Santa Claus, then, aren't you?"

Mr. Walter Blanchard, musical director, broke into a hearty laugh, which was echoed only faintly by Mrs. Grey, who interrupted it to speak haltingly, "But Mildred? I thought, with all her training—and her work—I cannot understand. It seems scarcely fair."

"Madam," the little man's voice was unexpectedly grave, and he spoke slowly, "to be a skilled and thoughtful musician is a good thing, a fine thing. But there are times—Christmastime is one of them—when it is finer, greater simply to make beautiful music for those who need it."

A Random Shot

Marion Hill

Tough times had come to the family of five, and they'd been forced to leave their beloved home and move far away. Now Christmas was nearing just as the last of their remaining money ebbed away.

What could four girls do to help their despairing mother?

* * * * *

The "Scavenger" had gone to bed, but as we knew from experience, far from being asleep, she was listening to every word of our conversation and was storing it in her memory with the intention of quoting it at some future time to our discomfort.

She was only twelve years old and, being the youngest, was doomed to run the family errands. Though she rebelled each time she was asked to go anywhere, in her heart she gloried in any chance to scour the neighborhood and find out whatever was new or interesting. In her innocent babyhood she had been christened Lillian, but when, as a growing child, tucks were let out, and she began to depend upon old iron, bottles, and the contents of the ragbag as the chief sources of her income—and consequently was forced to collect the articles of her trade with much unscrupulousness and energy—we bestowed upon her that eminently more descriptive title, the Scavenger.

By this time you have learned that we were poor. Mother was downstairs sewing and assumed we four girls had gone to

bed, but three of us sat before the dying fire and bemoaned our poverty. We were Vivian, Clara, and Nan. I am Nan, the eldest of the sisters. Vivian and I have no nicknames, but Clara is called "Herc," short for Hercules—a well-won honor bestowed upon her in recognition of her prowess in such feats as lifting the kitchen stove, moving the bookcase, or beating carpets.

"To be poor is hard, at any time," sighed she, "but it is doubly hard at Christmas. Here it is the middle of December, and we have not a dollar among us."

"My heart aches for Mother," said Vivian. "She is fretting herself ill over the bills."

"I should like to scalp the butcher!" murmured Herc, in serious meditation.

An odd sound from the bed, a half strangled sob, caused us to look at each other in surprise.

"What is the matter, darling?" asked Vivian, going over to the bed and trying unsuccessfully to lift from the Scavenger's face the bedclothes which were dragged over her features and clutched fiercely from beneath. "Tell your Vivian what troubles you, dear."

After being urged to several times, the grief-stricken one raised a corner of the bedclothes and sobbed forth in a roar of woe, "Mother *is* sick! And all because she has no money. Yesterday I went into her room for some pins, and I found her on her knees by the bedside, crying and praying—*praying in the daytime! Oww,*" and the long-drawn sob betrayed that in the last statement she fancied her recital had reached its acme of distress.

"Don't cry, little girl, don't cry. Things may grow brighter by and by," said Vivian soothingly, but her own voice trembled. In fact, the sudden tears also started in Clara's eyes and mine as we guessed at the suffering our little mother had so bravely kept from us.

Vivian brushed the damp hair from the child's forehead and petted her into a more resigned frame of mind. When she found out after a while that the much-comforted Scavenger was sobbing merely for her own private enjoyment and reveling in the way the bed shook with each convulsive throe, Vivian came back to her old seat by the fire and asked, "Is there *no* way in which we girls could make a little money and help Mother along? Is there *nothing* we can do?"

"We have not an accomplishment in the world," I said a little bitterly.

"Herc might give music lessons!" said a voice from the bed with a sobbing cackle of dismal mirth.

The sting of this suggestion lay in the fact that Clara (than whom no one had less ear for music) in moments of dejection was given to twanking viciously on an old banjo, which she played with so little melody and so much energy as to drive the rest of us to distraction.

Herc broke into an amiable burst of laughter, then sank back immediately into her former state of depression.

Vivian sighed wearily and fell into a reverie that must have been far sadder than we others could guess.

Two years before, she had been engaged to be married to a young man who was so affectionate, so boyish, so full of fun that he soon won Mother's heart as completely as he had won Vivian's. As for us girls, we simply adored him.

"Brother Bob," for so we soon learned to call him, was summoned to England just three months before the day set for the wedding, to take possession of a fortune which had been left him unexpectedly. And then came the sad, sad news that on the vessel's return trip he drowned.

After that news, everything went wrong with us. We had to give up our Philadelphia home and move to San Francisco, expecting in a vague way to do better, but we were disappointed,

and only by severest economy were we enabled to keep a roof over us. Poverty is a skeleton that may be kept decently in his closet until Christmastime; *then* he comes forth and rattles his bones under one's very nose.

Indeed, the prospect was so dismal that it actually prevented us three tired girls from going to bed. We sat around the grate, looking intently at the fire as if trying to wrest a helpful suggestion from the fast-dropping ashes.

This second silence had lasted fully ten minutes when it was again cheered by a speech from the bed.

"See here," said the muffled voice. "I have a splendid idea, but I am afraid you—you *things*—will laugh at me if you don't like it."

"Why, Lil, of course, we won't!" said Vivian reproachfully.

Thus encouraged, the flushed and blinking Scavenger struggled into a kneeling position and addressed us with dignity. "You know our old washerwoman, Biddy Conelly?"

Of course, we did and said so.

"You know the paper cake and boot button shop she keeps?"

"Well?"

"Biddy is laid up with rheumatism, and the shop is shut."

"*Well?*"

"Well!" defiantly, as the crisis grew nearer, "Why can't we keep the shop until Biddy grows better and make a kind of Christmas place of it with cornucopias and Christmas tree things and have lots of fun and earn lots of money?"

Silence reigned. Breathless and astounded, we could only look at each other.

Then what a gabble of tongues! What a deluge of "fors" and "againsts"! What a torrent of questions and answers! What a delicious flavor of romance! What a contagious ex-

citement and freshness there was about the whole plan!

"Shopkeepers? Delightful idea! We might be able to pay all the bills and buy Mother a new dress!" said Vivian.

"I shall be able to keep my rag money all for myself, and I'll buy a bicycle," said the sanguine originator of the plan.

"Let us go to bed and gain the strength to unroll the project before Mother in the morning," concluded I, with wisdom.

Well, we carried our point. Mother at first would not consent; but the gentleman who rented our front parlor spoke loudly on our side by deserting the premises without having paid his last month's bill, and we used this deplorable incident to such advantage that Mother finally gave in.

Two of us rushed at once to Biddy's, and had an entirely satisfactory interview with her. Not only did she refuse to charge us rent for the shop and stock on hand, but she lent us a little money that we might lay in goods of an essentially holiday nature.

There was much to be done before we could throw open our establishment to an indulgent public. At home, Mother and Vivian worked untiringly—Mother crocheting and knitting, Vivian dressing dolls and painting little pictures for our show window. At the store, Lil, Clara, and I were equally busy and afforded Biddy, who lived in the rooms above, much pleasing excitement.

Clara, especially, merited much praise. Slender and girlish as she was in figure, she performed many manly feats, especially in the way of carpentry, and when it came to cleaning, the rest of us were nowhere beside her.

"Cleanliness is the thief of time," she panted, "but it's the only way to be healthy, wealthy, and wise."

As we intended to be "shopkeepers" for two weeks only, and, moreover, as we were such comparative strangers in the

city that we had no arrogant acquaintances to shock, the day on which we opened our little store found us four of the most expectant, most excited, happiest girls in the world.

Oh, you *must* hear a short description of our dear shop! It was on Third Street, almost an hour's ride from our house. It had only one show window and was a bakery, a confectioner's, and a stationer's, all rolled into one. But our chief pride was in our Christmas goods and tree ornaments. We considered our assortment of dolls and our stock of tin toys unrivaled; and we reached our crowning holiday effect by means of wreaths and ropes of fragrant evergreen.

At the back, opening out of the store, was a small room, and before its bright fire we sat and chatted whenever we were off duty. We made fun of everything and everybody; we roared at the poorest jokes; we were in a touch and go state of good humor from morning till night. Indeed, we look back upon those days as the merriest of our lives.

Our first customer! The words send a thrill through me even now. We fought so for the honor of first standing behind the counter (before the arrival of any buyer, of course) that we finally drew lots for it, and the Scavenger won. She made us retire into the back room and closed the door; then she triumphantly mounted guard alone. The bell tinkled! A child came in! We three in exile pressed our faces to the curtained glass door and breathlessly watched the proceedings. Child pointed to a tin horse; Lil handed it to him; child nodded; handed it back; said something; Lil wrapped horse in paper; gave it again to child; child took laboriously a coin from his stuffed pocket; laid it on the counter; child went out.

Simultaneously we burst into the shop and cried, "Let us see it! Show us the money!"

"First blood for me!" shrieked the Scavenger, dashing a ten-cent piece into the till.

Vivian, who was bookkeeper, entered the ten cents amid frenzied rejoicings. Soon after her first sale, Lil shoved her head into the sitting room and observed with a quiet chuckle, "I say, Vivian, a young man was just straying past and caught sight of your paintings, and they were so bad they made him ill."

"They didn't," cried Clara indignantly.

"Did too. He gave one look and then reeled, positively *reeled* away."

Vivian was so used to having her pictures ridiculed that she merely smiled and said nothing.

Late in the afternoon Lillian and I were on duty together. We were very tired, all of us, for we had had an extremely busy day, the stream of customers being almost an unbroken one. Lest the uninitiated jump to the conclusion that we were on the high road to fortune, the explanation is necessary that very few of the purchasers spent more than a dime at a time. Often, indeed, the worth of a nickel sufficed for their modest needs. Often we suffered the shock of seeing them go out without having bought anything at all. To Lillian and me was granted the glory of having a customer out of the ordinary. He came at twilight, just before the lights were lit—an elderly looking, heavily bearded gentleman with a gruff voice. He glanced sharply at both of us and then said to me in a nervous, rambling way, "Er . . . ah . . . got any paper? Notepaper?"

"Yes, sir, plenty."

"Give me . . . er . . . five dollars' worth."

Five dollars' worth? I repeated in amazement.

"Um . . . yes."

When the enormous package was at last presented to him, he paid for it promptly but was not yet satisfied.

"Have you . . . any, well, er . . . any nice, first-class gold pens?" he asked, again in his uncertain fashion.

As he was looking directly at them, an answer was

unnecessary, so I silently placed the tray of pens before him. He took five, at two dollars each. I tied them up for him, blushing hotly the whole time and feeling very much ashamed, for I had come to the mortifying conclusion that he was throwing his money into our till from benevolent motives only and did not really need a solitary pen or a single sheet of paper.

"Nice store . . . very," he said, gruffly yet affably, catching the Scavenger's glassy and dismayed stare. "Am setting up a Christmas tree . . . will want *cartloads* of things. Have got . . . er . . . lots of children." Here he described with his gloved hand an immense arc in the air to illustrate the size and number of his children.

"All will have to have presents. Must go now. Will drop in again. Goodbye."

The door closed behind him. Lil and I, after an astounded look at each other, rushed into the little parlor to tell the girls.

"A nice sort of customer to have. I wish he would come again," said Vivian.

"He's going to; he said so."

"Was he young or old?" asked Hercules.

"Old," said I.

"Young!" said Lillian.

"He had a gray beard."

"Well, the eye part of him was young—real young," insisted Lil, and the subject was dropped.

When the eventful, delightful day ended, we ran upstairs to bid good night to Mrs. Conelly.

"It's a foine sthroke o' luck yez been havin'. Oi've sot by this windy, and it's wan hundhred and twinty-noine paple oi've counted thot's gone in an' out o' the sture," she declared.

"Impossible!" we cried.

"Oi've counted, and Oi know," she maintained stolidly.

"Sixty-noine gone in and sixty-nine cum out. Wan of thim thot wint in didn't go in at all, but kem up here and began pumpin' me about yez. Sorra a wurrud did Oi give him. Oi only tould him where yez lived, phwat yer names was, and how yez kem to be kapin' sture. Thin he tould me not to mintion him to yez, and not to tell yez whether he was a man or woman. An' Oi won't. Yez can't dhrag it out o' me."

"Did he—or she—have a long gray beard?" I asked anxiously.

"Sorra a hair on his face," she declared, adding, with a virtuous regard for truth, "barrin' an eyebrow or so."

As we could obtain no further information from her, we hurried homeward. It was charmingly dark, and we felt very independent and businesslike at being out at such an unusual hour.

Mother had a hot supper for us, and whether we ate most or talked most, she declared she could not tell.

When our hunger and excitement were both abated, we made the discovery that Mother had had a little excitement of her own and that she was trying to keep it from us. But we pounced upon her like a pack of hyenas. "Now, Mother, what is it? You are a bad hand at keeping a secret. Tell us. Out with it!"

Between laughing and crying, she finally told us all— that she had rented the two parlors to a very rich old gentleman who had not only given a high price for them but had positively paid three months in advance. She concluded by drawing a great bunch of money—real greenbacks—from her pocket and fluttering them above her head like little flags.

Our youngest relieved her feelings in a fantastic dance.

The next day at the store was a counterpart of the first, except that the reckless buyer did not appear. For three days he kept away, but he performed prodigies when he *did* return. Vivian, having stayed home with Mother, missed much of the

fun and had to hear secondhand a tale highly complimentary to herself, for the old gentleman bought all of her paintings, one after another, and stuffed them out of sight in his immense pockets. They seemed only to whet his appetite for more. "I will take . . . I want . . . give me that," and he pointed abruptly and without previous consideration to the most gorgeous doll in our collection.

The poor little doll-loving Scavenger sighed deeply as she beheld her favorite go headfirst into one of those rapacious pockets whence the paper-covered legs waved her a sad adieu.

Still unappeased, our customer demanded in his hearty way, "Now then, fetch me out Christmas tree fixings. Lots, please."

At this stage of events, Hercules, who was waiting upon him, blushed a painful red and said with meek determination, "No, sir, I'd rather not!"

"Bless my soul! What's the matter with you?" demanded he bluntly.

Through her desperation Herc answered honestly, "I don't think you really want anything you are buying, sir!"

He broke into a spasm of gruff, good-natured laughter but growled with evident sincerity that he needed all he had bought and more and would have to go elsewhere if she refused to supply him. And on her showing him what he asked for, he purchased articles enough to decorate a banyan tree and departed with the promise that he would "drop in tomorrow."

* * * * *

The night before Christmas! We had paid all the bills; we had secretly bought Mother and one another little presents; and the dear store which had enabled us to do so much was to pass into the hands of Biddy's cousin who had come to take charge on our departure.

The delightful nervousness of Christmas Eve was upon us all, and we all four were gabbing together in the center of the shop of which we were so soon to lose possession.

"Well, I just love the old man who bought such loads of things!" exclaimed Lillian. "We wouldn't have done half so well but for him."

"My goodness!" said Clara. "Speak of an angel, and you hear his wings!"

His wings made a lot of noise, for he burst in with his usual hearty clatter, but instead of dashing to the counter as was his wont, he stood looking steadily at Vivian who blushed and trembled under his gaze. And then, *then*—the cheery old fellow—what did he do but rush at our lovely Vivian and clasp her in his arms! It almost seemed that she had been put into one of those pockets, so completely did she disappear in the overcoat's embrace.

Before we, an indignant trio, had time to remonstrate, Vivian had torn herself away from him and was looking at him less in anger than in an undefined terror that yet was *not* terror.

"*Vivian! My Vivian!*" As his voice rang through the room, our pulses leaped with a strange remembrance, and Vivian, almost unconscious with joy, flung herself of her own free will into his arms.

Then what a crazy set we were! "Brother Bob!" "Dear Bob!" "Not drowned, but come to life again!" We shouted; we laughed; we cried. We all became like raving lunatics in our mad happiness. I found myself crying bitterly, all for no reason, over the Scavenger in a corner while *she* was shouting, "Bob! Bob! Bob!" at intervals like a demented calliope.

When we were the least bit calmed, Bob sent us into hysterics

again by putting his wig and beard into his pocket. And then we saw the dear remembered face!

"My own, my beloved Vivian!" he cried. The glad tears were running down his face quite as freely as down ours.

Vivian said never a word, but clung to Bob's arm like one in a dream. How we got into the street we never clearly remembered, but I know we found ourselves dashing homeward at a rousing pace, all talking together. We didn't want to be heard; we only wanted to talk. Still, we were keenly conscious of Bob's narrative. He told us how he lost track of us after he was saved from the lost ship, nobody seeming to know where we had gone; how, at the end of a two years' search, a faint clue had sent him to San Francisco; how he had seen in our shop window Vivian's painting of our old Pennsylvania home and had recognized it; how he had learned about us from Biddy; and how he had determined to mystify us and haunt the "sture" until he could get a chance of finding Vivian behind the counter.

"Here we are at home. Don't tell us any more," commanded Lil. "Save it for Mother."

On the doorstep we formed, in whispers, an elaborate scheme for Mother's mystification. Bob was to stay outside, while we went in and made Mother believe we had brought a homeless waif with us. Then she was to go out and bring him in to the light of her hospitable fireside, and he was to fall upon his knees and disclose himself—*tableau!* Bob assented with cheerful readiness, and we, after a violent ring at the bell, waited in palpitating expectation.

The door opened; we crowded past Mother and tried to force her away from the door while we all spoke at once, "Oh, let us tell you. We knew you wouldn't be angry, and we brought home with us a poor, old tramp with no home and no—" Here Mother gently freed herself, poked her dear, pretty head out of doors, and said placidly, "Come in, Bob."

We were petrified. She knew all about it!

"Don't try to deceive your poor old mother, girls," she said, throwing open the parlor doors, and—well, words fail me. At one end of the blazingly lighted room stood an immense Christmas tree, dazzling with candles and bearing on its drooping branches, beside myriads of costly gifts, every single article we had sold our "old man." It was like a child's dream of a tree. In an armchair by the fire sat Biddy Conelly, beaming happily upon us like a homely old fairy.

"Then Brother Bob is the 'rich old gentleman' who rented the rooms, and you knew it!" I cried, as light suddenly began to dawn upon me.

Through the blissful, but tear-dewed silence, came a still voice from the armchair, "Oi didn't know thot it wor the gintleman thot died, but Oi'm glad Oi held me tongue aboud him or—I ax yez—where would 'a' been the surproise of it?"

But Herc was looking admiringly at Mother and gasped at last, "Mama dear, I didn't know you could be *so underhanded!*"

The Cherry-Colored Purse

Susan Fennimore Cooper

Eleven cents. That was all Kitty had with which to buy her eleven Christmas gifts. Oh how frugal she'd have to be!

* * * * *

This story took place a long, long time ago when a penny bought a lot more than it would today.

* * * * *

A cherry-colored purse, not much the worse for wear, had been given to little Kitty Norton on her eighth birthday by her grandmama. Wrapped in soft tissue paper, this great treasure of Kitty's usually lay in a snug corner of her own particular drawer, but the day before Christmas of last year, the cherry-colored purse was not in its place. Little Kitty herself was seated, Turkish fashion, coiled up on the floor of her bedroom, and before her lay the purse. Kitty had come in from school in a prodigious hurry, with a bright, eager, busy little face. Throwing coat on one chair, hood on another, she made a dash at the old bureau. Yes, Kitty's bureau was old, and

so were the two chairs and the bedstead and the funny-looking three-cornered washstand. There was no carpet in Kitty's bedroom—the floor was painted. So, you see, this was not at all a fashionable house. But not a bit did Kitty mind that; her father was a wise and good country clergyman, but very poor.

For half a minute Kitty sat on the painted floor perfectly quiet, lost indeed in a very profound calculation. "Let me see," she said to herself. "I must first count over all the presents I've got to make. I mustn't forget anybody! There's Grandma and Papa and Mama—that's three—and sisters Bessie and Mary. Then there are the boys, Tom and Willie, and the baby— that will be eight presents. Then Biddy must have a present too—of course, she must! And I must have a real beautiful present for Aunt Lou, and I must have something for Cousin Kate too. Yes, that's it—eleven presents in all. Now let me see about the money!"

Kitty took up the cherry-colored purse and gave it an admiring look. One of the steel rings was pushed back, and a piece of money drawn out. It was a silvery penny. Kitty laid it on the floor. "That's the penny Mama gave me for taking care of the baby when Biddy was out." The little fat fingers went back into the purse again. A larger piece of money came out this time. "Two cents! Yes, Tom gave me those two cents on my birthday. Boys never *do* make the right kind of presents. But then they are only boys!"

The two cents were laid on the floor, and there was another dive into the treasury. Another penny came to light, not so bright and fresh as the first. It was laid by its companions on the floor. "Yes, that's all right. Four cents. That is all on this side. But there's silver in the other end of the purse!" exclaimed Kitty in a very important tone.

The steel rings were moved, and the little fingers went into the silver end of the purse. A piece of silver was brought to light and laid on the floor. "Yes, that's the three-cent piece Auntie gave me for picking strawberries one afternoon. But there's more silver yet."

Quite true; another tiny silver coin came to light. "This is the three-cent piece Papa gave me at the fair. I told him I'd rather have the money than the slice of cake. I had had one slice of cake, and I did want the money so bad for the little orphan children! I do love the orphans so! But, dear me! I am afraid I can't possibly spare even a single cent for the poor children now. I've ever so many presents to buy—just eleven presents. And let me see—just ten cents on the floor, and I'm sure there's one more penny in the purse. Here it is! Eleven cents in all, and eleven presents. I'm afraid I shall have to spend it all on presents!"

Twisting up her little mouth and wrinkling her little nose, Kitty sat fully half a minute lost in deep and silent thought, looking at the pennies on the floor. The secretary of the Treasury when studying the finances of the nation could hardly have looked more solemn. To pay the national debt is indeed a tremendous effort, but to purchase eleven Christmas presents with eleven cents is no trifle either, especially if one wishes to help the orphans too.

"Yes, it will *all* have to go for the presents. I can't spare one cent for anything else. I'm sorry about the orphans, but at Christmas it would be downright *cruel* not to give everybody a present. Dear Baby won't care much, but he *shall* have his own little present too. And they are all to be surprises! If it wasn't for that, I would talk to Grandma or to sister Mary about it. But nobody is to know anything about my presents. Tom says he peeped through the keyhole and saw all the presents. But he *couldn't* see mine, for I hadn't bought them. I'm going out to buy them now!"

And up jumped Kitty, gathering her money into the cherry-colored purse and dropping it into her pocket. "I wonder if my pocket will hold *all* the presents. Yes, the bundles won't be large. I think they'll *all* go into my pocket. Where's my list? I

had to write it out on my slate. Mama always writes her lists on paper, but I write *so big* Mama couldn't afford to give me paper enough, so I wrote it on my slate. I can't take the slate with me into the stores, so I'll read it over before I go."

And Kitty took her slate out of the drawer of the old bureau; it was covered with great scrawls which nobody but Kitty herself could have read. She understood it all, however, and having refreshed her memory, she put on coat and hood again, and was soon in the street on her great shopping expedition.

It was a pleasant afternoon, and the streets were full of people. Half of them seemed to be buying Christmas presents. It is pleasant to think how many of the men and women and children we meet in the streets in Christmas week are busy on the same happy errand. But I don't believe there was anyone in all that town who had eleven presents to make with so very few pennies as Kitty. But Kitty was a clever little business woman. She saw her way, or thought she did, through all difficulties. She felt sure of her eleven presents.

With the cherry-colored purse in her pocket, she went first to a great hardware store.

"I must go in here," said Kitty. And making her way through stoves and plows—all sorts of great ugly, useful things—and gliding between some tall, stout ladies and gentlemen who were making purchases, she reached a vacant spot at the counter. A clerk stood behind it. "Have you any small copper rings, sir?"

The clerk was an old gentleman with spectacles on, who looked very good-natured. Kitty saw him at church every Sunday.

"Do you have a wedding ring, my dear?" he said, as he opened a box full of copper rings.

Kitty blushed and smiled, but did not answer.

"Perhaps it is only for a female friend?" said the old gentleman again.

"It's a ring for a holder—a stove holder [pot holder]," said Kitty, timidly. "It's to hang the holder on the brass nail near the stove."

"A Christmas present, I see. And you've worked the holder, and it's for your mother," said this funny old gentleman as he wrapped up the ring in a thin bit of paper and gave it to Kitty.

"Yes, sir," said Kitty, whose eyes opened with astonishment at the old gentleman's knowing so much about the holder she had been working on so mysteriously.

From the hardware store she crossed the street to a dry goods shop, saying to herself, "Mama will have a *beautiful* present, and it only cost me one penny, for I had the worsted [yarn] and the canvas—Auntie gave me those ever so long ago."

The dry goods store was very much crowded indeed. Some little girls, friends of Kitty's, were there. She had to wait a long while before the clerk could attend her. But while talking to her little friends, she kept one eye on the counter, and presently, seeing an opening, she took courage and asked for some narrow blue ribbon. A box of ribbons was laid on the counter; she chose a piece of a pretty shade that was quite narrow.

"May I have a penny's worth of this ribbon?" asked Kitty very timidly, her heart beating with anxiety.

"If you'll pay for it!" said the clerk, looking cross and speaking in a rough, gruff voice.

"Oh, I've got the penny here," said Kitty, much relieved, and drawing out the cherry-colored purse, she took out a penny and laid it on the counter.

A little less than a quarter of a yard of the pretty blue ribbon was measured off (it was five cents a yard), and as the

clerk rolled it up and handed it to her, he thought to himself, *You're a strange customer*, but he didn't say so out loud.

"Now," said Kitty, skipping along, "I've got my beautiful present for Grandma too. Aunt Lou says it's a real beautiful pincushion, though it's not very big, but it is large enough to hang up near the looking glass where Grandma always hangs her cushion. It didn't cost me anything but the penny for the ribbon. That will make a beautiful bow and loop!"

Presently Kitty came to a bookstore. She went in and found it so crowded she could hardly make her way among all the people. They were buying pictures and books and music and knickknacks of all kinds. She had to wait some time, but at last her little face appeared above the counter, anxiously turned toward the clerk. Catching his eye, she asked for "some books," and then, coloring, added, "some *very little* books." It was not Shakespeare's or Milton's works that Kitty wanted. A small drawer full of very little books was placed before her. And now great was Kitty's perplexity. She would have liked to buy all the books. They all looked so interesting and inviting, with bright-colored covers and pictures. This present was for her brother Willie, a little boy seven years old and fond of reading. At last she chose for him a book with a red cover about birds and beasts.

"Is this one penny or two pennies?" asked Kitty with some anxiety.

"A penny," was the fortunate answer.

So Kitty handed over her two-cent piece and had the pleasure of receiving change for her purchase.

"I'm sure Willie will like that, because he likes to hear about animals," said the little sister to herself. "Now I have only eight more presents to buy!" And she went skipping along until she came to a shop where they sold a little of everything. Here she hoped to make a great many of her purchases. She scarcely knew what to ask for first; but edging her way among a row of ladies and children at the counter, she saw a parcel of worsteds [yarns] open before her. One skein of pink worsted [yarn], a lovely rose color, and one of sky blue, were chosen and paid for.

"These are for Aunt Lou and Cousin Kate," said Kitty to herself, as she laid down two cents and received the worsted [yarn] from the clerk.

"Will you please show me some marbles?" she said. A box of marbles of all sorts was placed before her—splendid alleys and bullies—very tempting, indeed, but, alas! those were much too expensive. So she asked how many common marbles she could have for a penny. "Five," was the answer. So she chose five of the best in the whole box as a present for her brother, Tom.

Then she picked out a pennywhistle for the baby, a little boy two years old. Her next purchase was a beautiful bodkin, looking quite silvery; and this actually cost only one cent more! It was for her sister Mary. Then in the next moment she bought a large darning needle for another penny; this was for her good friend Biddy. A handsome black-headed shawl pin was next purchased for sister Bessie—very cheap, indeed, at a cent; it looked as if it might be worth fully two cents!

By this time the cherry-colored purse was very nearly empty. There was but one cent left. Kitty looked at the tiny coin half regretfully—she had intended it for the little orphans. But then Papa—dear Papa—yes, it must all go for him! Papa's present was the most important of all. So Kitty asked if they had any penny penholders. Yes, a clean, fresh-looking one was produced. As the clerk was rolling it up, he asked Kitty if she needed a penholder to use in keeping her business accounts. This clerk belonged to Mr. Norton's congregation, and taught in the Sunday School; he knew Kitty very well. The little girl

laughed and said the penholder was for Papa. And she laid the last penny on the counter. The young man pushed it back. "Keep it for something else," he said, smiling.

Kitty looked up, surprised; she was bewildered. The clerk smiled more and more and pushed the penny toward her.

"Is it mine?" she asked. "And the penholder, too?"

Her friend nodded and turned to another customer. Kitty's heart gave a bound, and her face flushed all over. "Thank you, sir!" said Kitty in a voice that seemed very loud to her. The clerk smiled pleasantly in reply, and Kitty's eyes fairly sparkled as she dropped the penny into the cherry-colored purse again.

Oh, the little orphans won't lose the penny, after all! she thought to herself. And away she ran home as fast as her little feet could carry her.

There was no time to be lost, for the presents were all to be hung on the Christmas tree that evening. She rushed upstairs.

On the way she met her mother and said to her with an air of great mystery, "Please, Mama, don't let the children come into my room to disturb me. I'm going to label my presents!"

Mama smiled. No one disturbed her. The labels had all been written out the day before on scraps of paper cut from old envelopes which her grandmama had given her. They were all obliged to be very economical and saving in that family, for Mr. Norton's salary was very small. It took only a little while to wrap the presents up, each with its label pinned on it. The labels were all written in Kitty's best handwriting. In a jiffy the ring was sewed on Mama's holder, and the bow of ribbon on Grandmama's pincushion.

Then, with a joyful heart, Kitty carried the whole eleven presents down to Aunt Lou, who hung them on the tree!

* * * * *

There was not a happier little girl that Christmas Eve in all the country than little Kitty Norton. That is saying a great deal, but it is quite true. No doubt good Mr. Peabody felt happy when he gave away his millions to the poor people of London. Everybody who gives from the heart feels happy. But Mr. Peabody, with his millions, was not quite so happy, I fancy, as little Kitty with her eleven cents' worth.

Ermee's Christmas Doll

Alice Josephine Johnson

Ermee and Bertie, being orphans, were all each other had. Consequently, when Ermee was adopted and Bertie was not, much of the light in Ermee's world seemed to go out.

Finally, she came up with a plan.

* * * * *

It all happened so quickly that on looking back it seemed like a dream to the children. They had that morning invented a new play. Ermee was a great lady from the city who could play on the piano—a large wooden soapbox on which were rows of corncobs and cones for white and black keys. Bertie acted the admiring audience—an easy task, for it was his natural attitude toward his beautiful sister.

The audience was unexpectedly increased, however, by the arrival of a lady and gentleman who drove into the yard at that moment. The children had seen them pass the house the day before, and Amos, the hired man, had said they were "some of Mis' Tarbox's folks from New York. Awful rich, they say too," he added.

The strangers stopped a moment to watch the children before entering the house, and after their greetings, the lady asked eagerly of her hostess, "Who is that pretty child, Mrs. Willis?" with a nod toward the little girl.

Mrs. Willis explained that the children were two orphans. Their father had brought them to board with her nearly a year previous, but in the meantime he had died. His small life insurance was barely enough to provide for one of the children, much less two, but Mrs. Willis had determined to keep them with her if nothing better offered.

Before she had finished speaking, Mr. Leeds had read his wife's thoughts as her face kindled with excitement, and he was ready, as always, to anticipate her wish.

"You want to take the little girl, Nellie, do you?" he asked.

"Yes, Ned, can't we?"

"If you like, my dear," replied Mr. Leeds kindly, and his wife, thanking him with a smile, began to arrange with Mrs. Willis to take the child to New York the following day.

Ermee was called in and introduced to the pretty lady in the handsome gown and to the pleasant gentleman who at once produced a bag of candy from his pocket.

"He is never without that," laughed his wife, and Ermee privately decided that he was the kind of a man to know. She could not understand her good fortune when Mrs. Leeds asked her how she would like to go home with them and be their own little girl and have a doll and a doll's house and a pony and a real piano and other things too numerous and too bewildering for her to understand.

It was only after Mr. and Mrs. Leeds had gone and Mrs. Willis had begun to pack Ermee's belongings in the little half trunk which more than held them all, that the child realized that it was more than a delightful dream. Then she began to look grave.

"You can write little letters to us even now," said Mrs. Willis, "and after you have been to those fine schools, it will be no work at all to send us nice long ones, and Bertie will soon be old enough to write to you."

"Bertie!" exclaimed the child, aghast. "Isn't he going with me?"

She looked so pained that good Mrs. Willis hesitated, but on Ermee's repeating the question, she admitted reluctantly, "Why, no. They could hardly take you both, but Bertie shall stay with me, and you can come to see him in the summer, and they may invite him to New York sometime—who knows?"

"If Bertie is not going, then I won't go either," Ermee burst forth stormily.

"But it will be so much better for you," said Mrs. Willis.

"I don't care if it is," the child replied quickly.

"And so much better for Bertie," added Mrs. Willis.

"How?" asked Ermee.

"Because, dear, there is only a little money for both of you, but if these people take care of you, there will be all the more for Bertie."

This argument had its effect, as Mrs. Willis had foreseen it would, and Ermee rebelled no more, though it was hard for her to be comforted. But she promised Mrs. Willis that she wouldn't let Mr. and Mrs. Leeds know how grieved she was to leave her brother.

She kept her word, and when Mr. Leeds came for her he found her looking grave and pale, to be sure, but calm and quiet. When they drove away the tears came, but she cried softly and turned her head aside so Mr. Leeds wouldn't see her face.

Once on the train, there was much to entertain her, for railway travel was new to her.

When they reached Boston, after they had eaten lunch, Mr. Leeds walked with her over to a garden and took her to ride on a beautiful big boat made in the shape of a swan.

"Oh, how lovely this is!" she exclaimed in rapture, but she wished Bertie were there to enjoy it with her.

She wished it still more when they reached New York and she was made acquainted with her beautiful new home, which seemed like a glimpse of fairyland itself.

She had no chance to be homesick, there was so much to see and enjoy, and when she went to school, she soon had many friends among the children there. Indeed, Ermee made friends wherever she went, and they were of all ages and station.

Among her new friends was an old farmer, who drove into town every week and left fresh eggs and butter at Mr. Leeds's house. He was a sociable old fellow and used to stop for a chat as he made his weekly rounds. He took a great fancy to Ermee and often asked her if she would like to go home with him. "You can gather eggs and feed the chickens and help my wife about the house. Send her out to me, Mr. Leeds, when you want to get rid of her," he would say with a merry twinkle.

Ermee never knew whether he was joking or not and was at a loss at times to know how to reply to him. When she could, she avoided seeing him, and Mr. Leeds used to laugh at her for being afraid of Mr. Farrell.

"How can you treat him so, Ermee," Mr. Leeds once asked, with a laugh, "when he thinks so much of you and wants you for his own little girl? What if she should decide to leave us, Nellie?"

"I don't believe she will," replied Mrs. Leeds, with a fond glance at the pretty child who had completely won her heart.

"Well, we should have to hunt up someone to take her place, that's all," said Mr. Leeds. "We cannot be left alone again."

He little thought his bit of nonsense, which passed from his mind as soon as uttered, would bear the fruit it did. But the words sank deep into Ermee's mind. She had never been able to fully enjoy her lovely home, for the thought of her dear little brother, deprived of all the pleasures lavished upon her, saddened her loving little heart.

She was two years older than he, and after their mother died, her father had told her that she must be Bertie's "little mother." The fancy pleased her, and in her childish way she had shown a tender care of the little boy. Now it seemed to her that she had proved unfaithful in going where she had surroundings and belongings and enjoyments so far beyond anything that Bertie had ever known. In her unselfish little heart she often wished that Mr. Leeds had chosen Bertie. "He would have such good times here," she would often say to herself. She had even gone so far as to contemplate suggesting an exchange, and now a way seemed most unexpectedly opened, for Mr. Leeds had said that if she went away, he should have to get some other child. Old Mr. Farrell had often asked her to go home with him and be his little girl. She didn't really like the old man with his long, gray beard and hard, rough hands, his deep, gruff voice and odd ways, and most likely Mrs. Farrell might be worse, but she could be of use to them, and her going would leave a place open for Bertie. If she could only summon up courage to speak to Mr. and Mrs. Leeds about it!

She had been careful to obey Mrs. Willis's injunction not to let her kind friends know how hard it was to leave Bertie, and in consequence she had said so little about him they supposed she did not miss him. They were surprised, therefore, at an incident which occurred about this time and which bade fair to give Ermee the much desired opportunity of suggesting her plan.

They were out walking, when she suddenly gave a cry and ran after a little boy who passed them in the crowd. Mrs. Leeds followed her, saying, "You will get lost, dear, if you don't keep with us. What is it?"

"Oh, that little boy! I thought at first it was Bertie. See how much he looks like him!"

Her face was flushed with excitement as she gazed at the stranger, who stared in return, wondering what it meant.

Her eyes filled with tears when the child passed out of sight, and seeing Mr. and Mrs. Leeds exchange glances, she said quickly, "Oh, I am doing wrong! Aunty Willis told me I must not grieve for Bertie, when you were so good to me, and I promised I wouldn't talk about him."

"But we like to hear about your little brother. You shall talk about him all you choose," said Mrs. Leeds kindly.

"Oh, may I?" And the expressive face brightened and dimpled once more, as she prattled on about him in a way that went to the hearts of her hearers.

"He is so good and sweet; I am sure you would both love him," she said, with her happy smile.

"We do now, for his dear little sister's sake," Mr. Leeds replied.

"Oh, but he's ever so much nicer than I am, really," she said earnestly.

Mr. Leeds laughed as he replied, "I cannot believe that. Anyway, you are good enough for us, but we will take him when you go to Mr. Farrell's."

Ermee's eyes grew large. Her purpose was accomplished. And though her heart ached at the thought of leaving dear Papa and Mama Leeds, she did not hesitate. There was no chance to say more then, as they met a friend at that moment,

but she made up her mind to talk it over with them that very evening.

It happened, however, that on their return a telegram awaited them, announcing the illness of Mrs. Leeds's sister who lived in New Hampshire, and an hour later both Mr. and Mrs. Leeds were on their way to the station.

There seemed nothing to do but await their return, but a letter she received from Mr. Leeds changed Ermee's plans. He wrote that as his sister-in-law was better, he and his wife had planned to stop over a day, on their way home, and go to see Bertie. They were to return the last of the week, reaching home on Christmas Eve. Quick as a flash came the thought: *Now he can bring Bertie home with him, if I go to Mr. Farrell's.* And a moment later she began to write with a hand which trembled with excitement:

> Dear Papa Leeds:
> You said once that you would take Bertie if I went away, and so I am going to Mr. Farels. Of course I would rather stay with you, but Bertie is litler than me, and Papa used to say I ought to think more about his having a good time than of having one myself. I can't at your house, for I have all the good times, and Bertie don't have any.
> I hope it will be all rite, and you will bring Bertie home. I send lots of kisses to you and dear Mama Leeds.
> Your loving,
> Ermee

When Mr. Farrell came next day, the little girl was waiting to meet him, and when he called out, after his usual custom, "Going home with me today?" he was gratified to have her reply, "Yes, if you will take me."

Mr. Leeds had promised the old man that Ermee should visit him some time, so he supposed she had permission to go, and so did Norah, the maid, and no questions were asked.

When Ermee spoke about her trunk, both Norah and Mr. Farrell agreed, with a laugh, that he could get it the next week. Norah packed her little bag for the night, thinking the child would probably be homesick before morning.

Homesick indeed she was at the mere prospect of leaving her dear home, but she girded up her courage, thinking of Bertie and the good times that awaited him.

The drive out to the farm was a pleasant one, and the house not unattractive. The same could not be said of Mrs. Farrell, however. She was a rather peculiar old woman, abrupt in speech and very deaf.

She was surprised to see her husband bringing a child home and inquired who she was.

When Mr. Farrell explained, she looked rather dubiously at Ermee and said, "Well, you'll find things different here from what you've been used to at Mr. Leeds's great, beautiful house."

After supper, for which Ermee had little appetite, she timidly asked Mrs. Farrell if she might wipe the dishes. To her relief, the offer was taken kindly, and when the old lady saw how deft and careful the child was, she patted her on the head approvingly. It was evident that Ermee had risen in her estimation.

In the evening Mr. Farrell read his paper, and his wife slept in her chair. Ermee could not help thinking regretfully of the happy evenings at Mr. Leeds's home, with music and games and a good night frolic to end with.

There was nothing pretty to look at in the large kitchen which the Farrells used for a dining room and sitting room too,

and the only books were a town history and a dictionary.

She was glad when Mrs. Farrell woke and announced it was bedtime. She lost no time in going to sleep, and slept so soundly that when she woke next morning, she was surprised at her unfamiliar surroundings and was puzzled for a minute, to know where she was. Then it all came back to her, and she broke into a little sob in spite of herself. But there was nothing to do but make the best of it, and, like the brave little girl she was, she resolutely dressed herself and hurried to the kitchen to see if she could help Mrs. Farrell.

After breakfast, she went to the henhouse with Mr. Farrell, and there she found much to entertain her. The day dragged, however, and by night she was thoroughly homesick. The next day was worse, and that night was Christmas Eve too. She curled herself up on the old lounge in the corner of the kitchen and cried herself quietly to sleep.

She knew no more till morning, and when she woke, thinking with a pang that there was no stocking and no presents, and, in fact, no Christmas, she suddenly stared about, amazed to find herself in her own little bed in the pretty room which Mrs. Leeds had fitted up for her. How came she there? Was it a dream or was it magic?

As she turned her head, there stood dear Mama Leeds by the bedside, smiling down upon her and wishing her a "Merry Christmas." What a hug and a kiss Ermee gave her, and then asked, thoroughly mystified, "But how did I get here?"

"Papa drove out for you last night, and you were so sound asleep you never wakened when he bundled you up and put you in the carriage, nor when I undressed you here. But I know my little girl has been homesick. I saw traces of tears on your cheeks. The idea of being away on Christmas Day! How could you run away as you did?"

"Oh, but Bertie! I must go back, if they will take me. *Won't you take Bertie?*"

"We will talk about that later. Now we must hasten down to the library. Papa is all impatient to have you see your gifts."

"But I didn't hang up my stocking," said Ermee dubiously.

"Oh, but we did for you," called out Mr. Leeds, who, tired of waiting, had come after his little girl. And, catching her up on his shoulder, he ran down the stairs with her, laughing like a boy.

"The biggest present won't go into the stocking, after all," said Mr. Leeds.

"Oh, is it another doll?" queried Ermee. "I hope it's a boy doll!"

Mr. and Mrs. Leeds both laughed at this, and as they entered the library, Ermee heard an odd little sound she did not understand, and she wondered if it came from some new toy.

In one corner stood a tall pasteboard box on end.

"Your present is in that," said Mr. Leeds. "Open it carefully."

In a moment she had the cover off—*and there stood Bertie!*

With a cry of delight, she had him in her arms, while he, half smothered with kisses, made several attempts to call out, "I've come to stay! And you're to stay too!"

When at last she understood him, she stared in wonder at Mr. and Mrs. Leeds as she asked, "You don't mean you're going to keep us *both?*"

"That is just what we mean," they answered in joyful chorus.

"And I needn't go back to Mr. Farrell's?"

"Well, I should say not! Don't ever mention such a thing to me again," said Mr. Leeds with mock gravity, and then putting an arm around each of the children, he said tenderly, "No, darling, you are our own dear little girl for now and always, and Bertie is to be our little boy. Had we known how you felt about him, we would have had him here long ago, but 'better late than never.' And now for the happiest Christmas Day that any of us has ever had!"

And so indeed it was. And, as in the old fairy tales, "they all lived happily ever after."

The Snowbound Santa Claus

Izola L. Forrester

The Pacific Overland Express engineer labored hard to get the train through the drifting snow. Finally, the train stopped and moved no more.

Mr. John P. Ridley, in his private car, was angry. In time, that anger turned into boredom. He decided to explore.

* * * * *

The Pacific Overland Express, from Omaha to the coast, stopped short with a slow, reluctant jerk. For more than ten miles, since noon, it had tried to make its way through the snow bergs that lay in huge drifts on the track, and now it gave up the fight and rested at the eastern base of Great Bear Pass.

Nell blew on the frosted window pane until she had melted a peephole to look through.

"Just mountains and mountains everywhere," she announced sadly, and four other young Harrisons listened in doleful sympathy. Christmas in a snowed-up car would be something dreadful.

"It's five o'clock now," said Max, "and the conductor says we won't be out before tomorrow, maybe, because they've got to telegraph for a snowplow to help us out."

Curled together in a disconsolate heap on one seat, Benjy hugged Tomikins up close, and they sobbed in united woe.

"No candy or turkeys or ballses, or dollies, or anysing," cried Tomikins.

"And no Santa Clauses too," added Benjy with a fresh howl.

Even Jeanette, as big sister, felt the tears gather slowly in her eyes in spite of her fifteen years, as she thought of the thirty-six miles that lay between them and Silver City.

"Will Santa Claus find us 'way out here?" asked Nell.

"Sure he'll find us," promised Max valiantly. "He'll make a beeline right over the mountains with those ponies of his—"

"Reindeerses," prompted Benjy, sitting up and taking an interest in life once more.

"Don't you suppose that Papa's beginning to worry about us, Jeanie?" asked Max.

Jeanette nodded her head. She knew if she tried to talk she would curl up in a heap like the twins, and have a good, hard cry.

At the end of the train, in the private car *Pocahontas*, sat Mr. John P. Ridley. It did not please Mr. Ridley that the Pacific Overland Express should be held up by a snowstorm. He believed that a properly conducted railroad should be equal to any snowstorm.

He kept his private porter busy running back and forth through the train, finding out what chances there were of getting through Great Bear Pass that night. It appeared that Mr. Ridley was especially anxious to get through that night for two reasons. The boxes and numerous small pieces of baggage that were stacked in one end of the car explained one of these reasons. The explanation of the other Mr. Ridley reserved for himself, for the telegraph operator back at Barker Junction, and for Warren, general manager of the Lakota mines in Silver City.

He was sorry for Harrison. He was a hard worker and thor-

oughly competent, but they needed a younger, quicker man as assayer at the Lakota mines. Harrison was, if anything, too painstaking. He experimented. Also, he was strictly conscientious. If it had not been for the coming deal in the Sunset mine, he might have kept him, but a thing like that needed a different sort of man. Not that it wasn't a "square deal." He believed himself that the Sunset was a good thing and only half developed, but so far the output had not justified the price he had put on it. In case of questions asked by the buyers, he did not want exactly a false report made by the assayer, but he did want a man who could see beyond the specimens in his hands and who would look after the interests of his employer enough to prophesy favorably on the future of the Sunset. Harrison was not good at prophesying.

Therefore a telegram had gone forward from Barker Junction which rendered the position of assayer vacant, and Mr. Ridley was very anxious to arrive in Silver City in time to meet the new assayer from Butte and instruct him on a few minor points of prophesying before the buyers for the Sunset should interview him.

When six o'clock came, he had his private dinner prepared in his private kitchen by his private chef, and he enjoyed it as well as his dyspepsia [indigestion] would permit him to enjoy anything, while in the cars ahead the general public rummaged in lunch boxes and baskets and shared with one another remains of cold chicken and sandwiches in philosophical merriment over the situation.

At half past eight, Mr. Ridley found his privacy growing monotonous. On Christmas Eve, in a snowbound train stranded in the heart of the Rockies, privacy is a bore, and so Mr. Ridley took a stroll through the train.

He found relief for a while in the smoking compartment of the first sleeper. There were several persons aboard the train who recognized the value of Mr. Ridley as a fellow passenger and were glad to make him welcome.

He had noticed, in passing through the sleepers, a rather noisy crowd of youngsters who were singing, playing games, and otherwise having a very jolly time.

It was after eleven when he left the smoking compartment. On his way back through the cars, the conductor met him and explained apologetically that the wires were down for several miles ahead in the pass, and it had been necessary to send back to Barker Junction in order to telegraph ahead for a snowplow. It might be several hours before they could go on—possibly not before the next morning.

Mr. Ridley was annoyed. As he went on through the narrow, curtained aisles of the sleepers, he felt vaguely resentful toward the whole system—railroad, snowstorm, passengers, and all—as a combined force of circumstances that could detain a man like John P. Ridley against his will. Suddenly he stopped short before Section 4 in the third sleeper. The two berths were made up, and they were close quarters too. In the upper one slept Max and the twins, Benjy cuddled up crosswise at the foot, and in the lower berth were Nell and Jeanette.

But all that Mr. Ridley saw was a row of stockings pinned up on the long curtains, like misplaced tails on a [pin the tail on the] donkey sheet. He stared at them through his eyeglasses thoughtfully. Two

small ones just alike, well darned around the toes and heels, one long, double-kneed one for a boy who might possibly play marbles, and two fine-ribbed ones with small feet.

After a minute's inspection, Mr. Ridley walked back to the end of the car and had a talk with the porter. When he had finished, he knew the personality of each stocking and the requirements of its owner. And then a very curious thing happened on the Pacific Overland Express. Back and forth between the third sleeper and the private car Mr. Ridley's private porter marched, his arms full of boxes and parcels, and when it came to opening them before Section 4, Mr. Ridley himself took a hand.

When the five stockings were full and bulged out at the tops, there were other parcels placed cautiously in the little hammocks that hung at the head and foot of the lower berth, and Mr. Ridley caught a glimpse of Nell's brown pigtails and Jeanette's yellow curls lying side by side on the pillow. When he returned to the private car after all was done, he was smiling comfortably to himself and had forgotten all about the wretched facilities of railroads for dealing with snowstorms. At home there were two heads, very similar to those in Section 4, waiting for Papa to come. That was the first reason why Mr. Ridley wanted to get over Great Bear Pass that night.

But just as the private porter gathered up the last pieces of string and paper from the aisle and started away after Mr. Ridley, Max's head appeared at the curtain opening of the upper berth. His hair was standing on end as only the hair of a pillow-tousled boy's can, and his eyes were round with sleepy, surprised amazement when he saw the bulging stockings.

In half a minute he had dropped from the berth, and a small white ghost in baggy nightclothes stole through the cars after Mr. Ridley and never stopped until the vestibule door of the *Pocahontas* shut out the world from its privacy.

At half past seven on Christmas morning, the snowplow

came through Great Bear Pass. The blizzard had stopped, and it was clear and cold. A committee of five waited for admittance in the vestibule of the *Pocahontas* while Mr. Ridley bathed, shaved, and dressed. It was a joyous, excited committee. Max led as guide, with Nell hugging his shoulder, and Jeanette tried to hold the twins in check, until finally the private porter ushered them in past the tiny kitchen and pantry, all shining brass and tiles, past the little compartment dining room, into the parlor section, with its dark green hangings and deep, low willow chairs, its bookcases, and piano, and broad windows.

Mr. Ridley rose from his desk to greet them. It was an awkward moment. Max and the girls waited doubtfully for each other to speak, until Tomikins broke the ice.

"Merry Cwismus!" he said.

"The same to you, sir," responded Mr. Ridley, a twinkle gleaming in his eyes. "Merry Christmas to all!"

Then Jeanette began, "We came because we wanted to thank you—"

"For being Santa Claus—" added Nell, eagerly.

"I saw you," exclaimed Max, forestalling any possible disclaimer. "I looked over the top of the curtains. My, but you just ought to have seen the kiddies when they found those music boxes!"

Christmas breakfast is a lonesome affair all by one's self. There were five guests in Mr. Ridley's dining room, and it was such a merry, delightful breakfast that no one noticed the time until the train began to move slowly forward.

"We're going!" shouted Max joyously. "'Rah! I really believe that Papa stayed in the depot all night."

"Are you going to Silver City?" asked Mr. Ridley.

Of course, they were. Why, didn't he know that before? Individually, and in chorus, they all told him how it had happened. "Way back when the twins were only a year old, the dearest little mother in the world was called to rest, and since then they had lived in Chicago with Grandmother Wilcox until Papa could take them all. It had been a long time to wait— almost three years—and they had been rather poor too."

"Not raggedly poor," protested Nell. "Just shiny."

But now everything was changed. Max's brown eyes sparkled with sturdy pride as he told how his father was assayer at the Lakota silver mines and how they were the finest mines in Colorado. Perhaps Mr. Ridley had heard of them. It appeared that Mr. Ridley had—slightly. It was a fine position, Max assured him, and steady too. That was why Papa had sent for them all to come to him, because he was sure it would last. And it wouldn't be hard at all, because Jeanie was going to be housekeeper, and they would all help her; and last of all, they just wanted to tell Mr. Ridley one thing—there wasn't a single father in the whole world quite as splendid as the one who was waiting for them in the depot at Silver City.

Mr. Ridley listened, a twin on each knee, and smiled. When breakfast was over, Jeanette said they must go back, because the kiddies were clamoring for the music boxes. So they waved their hands to him from the vestibule and called "Merry Christmas!" And after they had gone, Mr. Ridley went and stood before one of the car windows, looking out at the flying stretches of pine-dotted mountainside.

Finally he turned to his desk. A pad of telegraph blanks lay on it, and he wrote a message and called the private porter.

"Send that as soon as we reach Crescent," he said.

It was the last gift from Santa Claus, and Warren, general manager of the Lakota mines smiled when he received it. It read,

Retain Harrison.
J. P. Ridley.

Where Journeys End

Beth Bradford Gilchrist

Mary Strong had experienced everything in life and in travel but this—she had never known what a home was.
It seemed almost too good to be true.

* * * * *

It would not surprise me to see this virtually unknown ninety-two-year-old Christmas/motherhood/family story become a classic. Because of its length, *St. Nicholas* editors spread it out over two issues. It took only one reading to convince me that this story *had to be* the capstone of this collection.

* * * * *

Chapter I

The letter redirected at her New York school had said pleasantly:

My dear Mary—yes, my dear Mary—for, though I have never seen you, your mother and I were school girls together, which surely entitles me to call her daughter what I please—can you come to us for the Christmas holidays? I will not deny that this eleventh hour invitation means exactly what you will surmise: failure of an expected guest. Repay my honesty, if you can, by your alacrity. The car will meet the train which I have marked. With plenty of young people in the house, I think we can promise you a cheerful week, possibly indeed some little excitement. And surely my daughter and your mother's should know each other!
Cordially, your mother's friend and yours,
Alicia Coleman White

Established in her parlor car, magazine in lap, cushion at feet, Mary Strong was not thinking of the letter. Neither was she thinking of her father's elderly cousin, the family hotel, and the dull games of checkers from which she had fled. Sixteen years of wandering with a father and mother who pursued around the world a will-o'-the-wisp of health had accustomed the girl to taking things as they came, for better or worse. Steamers and railway trains, summer camps and boarding schools, east, west, and overseas, held no surprises for her. She had grown used to meeting strange people, falling into step with them for a few days or a few weeks, and passing out of sight of them as easily. Therefore she speculated little on the household to which she was going. Alicia Coleman was one of the few names connected with her mother's youth which she had heard her mother mention. There appeared to be a daughter. A son? More than one? "Alicia's houseful of boys" returned as a hazy memory. A recent letter of her mother's had mentioned hearing, through a mutual friend, of the engagement of a niece of Mrs. White who lived with her at Crawford. "The little one she called 'Pet.'" What was the daughter's name? Alice? Mary's recollections appeared scanty. Some faint curiosity stirred in her mind regarding Christmas outside a hotel or school. Life in a private house must in some ways be different, she supposed, from life as she knew it. Mary Strong had never experienced

a home in her life. She knew nothing about homes.

So she had a perfect right to be bored, sitting in the train two days before Christmas, idling through the pages of her magazine. Affection gives zest to life, and Mary's affections had never been allowed time to become rooted. She knew no ties, deep and far-reaching and strong— ties with a tug to them. Even with her father and mother it had always been touch and go. In her correctly tailored blue suit with her becoming Parisian hat, she looked capable, carefully bred, charming, but she had an unwarmed look. Nothing about her suggested that she was used to the embraces of mother's arms or the hugs of brothers and sisters. To shake her out of her cosmopolitan ruts and show her the breadth and height and depth of the things that she did not know, she needed to be taken up by life and dropped into the midst of a big, quiet, homey kind of adventure.

The adventure was on the way. It could not very well have happened; nevertheless, it did happen—one of those incidents that prove the strangeness of truth. It did not begin pleasantly. It involved an accident on a connecting road, vague delays, a missed train, and four tedious hours at an impossible junction feted with fast-falling snow. The junction had but one redeeming feature—a college boy. Without appearing to do so, Mary inspected him. She liked his laugh, his voice, his face, clean cut and strongly modeled, lightened by the twinkle in his eyes. She liked the breadth of his shoulders and the lithe ease of his athletic body. Best of all she liked the way he carried himself—collegiate probably. Other people liked it too; tired eyes brightened. A child or two got mixed up with the zest and energy of the boy and his friends; smiles grew to laughter. Then the collegians disappeared, and Mary herself annexed a small boy and girl for a walk through the village. Once annexed, they stuck like flies to a honey pot. Even after the train had roared out of the darkness, they murmured, "Go on," whenever she drew breath. Mercifully, they left at an early station.

But the train had been late. Moreover it had no parlor car, and it stopped at every hen roost. And Mary had made an early start. She consulted her watch and her timetable. It would be nine o'clock when she reached Crawford. A yawn refused to be diverted. The rattle and swing of the train lulled her. Despite herself, her eyelids drooped. Once or twice she nodded. She rolled her coat into a ball and pillowed her head on it. Between her catnaps the brakeman bawled unintelligible stations. Drowsily she wondered what he said. She was too sleepy to look up her timetable again.

"Hatley! Hatley!"

There was no mistaking Hatley. Hatley. East Crawford, Crawford. Her station was still two stops away. The man would call it with just that lift and fall of his voice, she supposed. Crawford! Crawford! She practiced it sleepily in imagination.

She woke with a sense of having done more than lose herself in a moment. She had been dreaming. For an instant, she did not know where she was. The wheels were groaning to a standstill. Outside her window glimmered the dim lights of a country station. In her ears resounded the brakeman's shout. His stressed syllables resolved themselves in her brain into the two for which she waited. Unmistakably he was calling Crawford.

Afterward she remembered jumping up, half awake, hurriedly collecting her things, stumbling down the aisle to the door, and stepping down, still sleepily, into snowy blankness. Behind her, the train began to move again. With the sound of its wheels, the cold air stung her brain to horrid activity. Could she have got off at the wrong station?

"This way, Miss. I'm to take you up."

It was all right then. Mechanically she extended her back to the fur-coated man.

"Have you a trunk?"

"Not on this train. I could not find it at the junction."

"Better give the check to someone at the house, then."

Beside the wooden platform glimmered the long dark body of a limousine. Mary Strong settled down in its warm rugs, comfortable in body and mind. Mrs. White had written that the car would meet her.

"Hello, John!" A voice struck familiarly on her ears. "Going to take me up too?"

So the collegian with the jolly laugh belonged in Crawford. Was he one of "Alicia's boys"?

Mary had little time for speculation. The car drew up before a brightly lighted house. The collegian jumped down from the driver's seat and opened the door for her. At the top of the steps stood a girl of about Mary's age. Her face was joyous with welcome. Her hands closed on the guest's eagerly.

"Oh, I'm so glad you're here at last!" she said. "I've always heard so much about you."

Chapter II

In the hall Mary Strong looked about her with covert curiosity. She saw everything without appearing to see anything except her happy young hostess. Mary thought she had never been in any place that looked in the least as this house did on its very threshold, and she wondered why. Had she but known it, the house was quite an ordinary house. To Mary it appeared an extraordinary place. The sheer livableness of it warmed her, as did the smile of the girl whose tongue ran glibly on.

"It was lovely of you to come! I'm Sally—we needn't waste

Helen Mason Grose

time being formal, need we?"

"Not if you will call me Mary."

"Mary? Oh, I like Mary. I'm glad you call yourself Mary. I didn't like your other name."

It gave Mary a fellow feeling to find another girl who disliked "Grace."

"My cousin, Bob Travers. What a pity that you didn't know each other!"

"If I'd known you were you," said the collegian, "I'd have scraped acquaintance."

"I wish you had. Wasn't that junction fearful?"

"The limit! Seems to me, Sally, Mrs. Lane might have told John to run down with the car and bring us up."

Sally laughed. "I think it's quite nice enough of her to tell us to use it today and tomorrow just as though it were our own. But aren't you both hungry? Will you go upstairs before supper, Mary? I forgot to ask about your trunk."

"It hasn't come yet." Mary repeated her explanations.

"The blue room, Bob," Sally directed, as he picked up Mary's bag.

"You haven't told us yet," he said, "where everybody is. I want Aunt Barby and Nell."

Sally turned to Mary. "He has called Mother 'Aunt Barby' ever since he was a little tad. Now neither of them will hear of any other name. She's in the city, Bob, with Nell, buying Nell's trousseau. They hoped to get back tonight, but they didn't quite finish. Tomorrow, we *shall* be busy. Father went up to Edgerton to see about flowers. He and Jim come down at midnight. Tracy is out doing errands. He hoped to get back in time to meet Mary's train. Midget and Molly have gone to Mrs. Lamb's to see about cakes. Katie is doing *the* cake, of course. And the children are in bed. There, that accounts for us all. Here is the blue room, Mary. Mine is just beyond

this wall. As soon as you're ready, come down, please. I know you're starved."

The blue and white room folded a bewildered girl within its crisp daintiness. A wedding! So that was what Mrs. White had meant by her vague reference to excitement. But how odd to invite an utter stranger to a wedding, even if she was the daughter of an old friend. Nell was the niece's name—Bob Travers's sister—formerly called "Pet." The "young people"—Tracy, Jim, Bob, Midget, Molly, Sally—what a family for nicknames! Even "Aunt Barby"! And what a darling room! Mary had never loved a room in her life. She hadn't known that it was done. Rooms were for shelter—mere conveniences, made to sort people out in. But at sight, tiny as it was, she loved this room.

In the dining room, Bob Travers was saying to Sally, "So that's the girl with the jaw-breaking name. You didn't introduce her, I noticed."

"Why, Bob! Indeed, I—"

"No, you didn't. Introduced *me* all right. Only 'Mary'ed her. I'll 'Mary' her too. Think she'll let me?"

"Of course not—so soon as this."

"You bet I won't call her the other thing. Not your Uncle Robert. Good looker, isn't she?"

"Bob, she's lovely! And her clothes!"

"They'll pass muster. Why didn't anybody have her here before?"

"Mother's tried, plenty of times, but something always interfered. Remember, Bob," Sally twinkled at him, "you're going to be busy tomorrow."

"She's going to be busy too—helping me."

Mary stood on the threshold, but had not heard his remark. "I didn't know they were going to be married so soon," she said.

"Nobody did," Sally told her promptly. "Please sit here. You like chocolate, don't you? Four days ago a night letter came from Grant Franklin. He was ordered to South America, sailing Saturday from New York to be gone a year, and would Nell be married right now and go with him? Of course, she thought at first she couldn't possibly get ready, but it made her sick to think of letting him go off so far alone. The things we had ready—tablecloths and napkins and towels—wouldn't help her in South America. Then Mother said, 'Nell, dear, you and I will go to the city and buy what you need.' They're even getting the wedding dress. And it's our job to trim the house tomorrow. We always do it anyway at Christmastime. Grant comes at five; the wedding is at eight tomorrow night."

"Tomorrow night!" gasped Mary.

Sally nodded excitedly. "Christmas Eve. Didn't Mother tell you? She wrote again after the telegram came."

"What Aunt Barby didn't tell, you've made up for by now, Sally," said Bob. "I always forget between vacations just how much information you can squeeze into a minute."

"The second letter never reached me," Mary told them.

Then Midget and Molly came in, and there were more greetings, more voices repeating Sally's friendly "Mary." "It's so much simpler than remembering always to say 'Miss.' "

"It is pleasanter," smiled Mary. She was so used to the sound of her last name that its absence in this house chimed with the exhilarating strangeness of everything about her.

"Let's make a rule!" cried Sally. "A Christmas rule. May we, Mary? Nobody shall call her anything but Mary, not a person in the house. It will make it so much more homey."

Bob turned to the guest ceremoniously. "Do you second the motion?"

"Yes, I second the motion."

"All in favor—unanimous vote! All handles to be permanently mislaid from now on. Will you help me rig out the house with evergreens tomorrow morning, Mary?"

"Surely I will."

"Surely you will—what?"

"Surely I will—Bob."

"Done. Ice broken, gone to smash. Hello, Tracy, old boy. Let your grandfather grip your hand. Having a tryout for Santa?"

It had all been like that, Mary thought that night, as she snuggled down into the little white bed in the lovable room—all jolly, friendly, and gay, and very new to her. It was like that the next morning, from the moment when she struggled up through folds on folds of sleep and descried two small white figures standing beside her bed, to the time when Sally's father's gravely smiling, "Mary it shall be, then," drew her within the breakfast circle as one who "belonged." He was dignified to look at, was Sally's father, but Mary had not been at table five minutes before she learned that he was as big a boy as any there. Gradually she pieced together relationships. Jim—huge of body and merry of eye—and tall, stately Midget were cousins to little Tom and Marian, to cordial Sally, and piquant Molly, and grave, dark, homely Tracy with the face that made you want to know him, but they were not brother and sister to Nell and Bob. These two stood for another branch of the family tree, Mary decided. She did not like to ask. Asking would reveal too dense an ignorance, and already her ignorance appalled her. Why had she never thought to question her mother about those old girlhood friends of hers? Names, whose identity it was assumed she knew, flashed from mouth to mouth. Her ignorance reflected on her mother's constancy to old ties, and suddenly Mary became passionately jealous of her mother's good repute.

"Everybody help trim," Molly was saying. "We simply must have the house done before Mother and Nell come at noon."

"Come along, Jim," said Tracy. "Let's be off for a last load

of green. You have a trunk check, haven't you, Mary? We'll bring your trunk along when we come back."

Five minutes later Mary descended the stairs into a tangle of ground pine and holly. "I can't find it," she admitted. "I never did such a thing in my life before as to lose a check. I'm thoroughly ashamed. But I took the number. Father impressed on me that I must always know the number of my check."

"He did, did he? You've a fairly long memory."

"Oh, I wrote it down."

"I didn't mean that! You've a pretty long memory to remember his saying it."

She looked puzzled.

"Come along and help me do the right thing by this window, Mary," called Bob.

"Guess I can get it by the number," Tracy told her. "More errands. Molly? Ready in a jiff, Jim."

The big fellow, leaning against the stair rail beside her, surveyed Mary smiling. "So you're 'Marcia's little cousin.' I'd a notion you were a tiny thing."

"I'm not very big beside you. But—'Marcia's little cousin'?"

"We always called you that. Come to think of it, Marcia was some kind of a thing-in-law to your father, wasn't she? Coming, Trace."

Marcia! Mary searched her memory. What had her father once said of a relation or near-relation other than the checker-playing cousin? But was her name Marcia? It was dreadful to be a girl who didn't know her own people.

Bob pranced to the foot of the stairs. "Won't you please get onto your job? Midget says my window's a nightmare."

Mary smiled and went with him. Ground pine passed through her fingers. Holly pricked them. In the rising tide of joyous excitement she forgot the surprising number of things she did not remember—the relatives, her own and others'—

to whom she was a stranger. Something within her seemed to be growing, putting out little tendrils like the tendrils of a vine that curl and cling. For the first time in her life, she knew what it would be like to care for one spot of earth more than you cared for any other spot. Wholeheartedly she echoed Sally's rapturous exclamation, "Don't you love it? Don't you?"

"No other house I was ever in has the smell of ours at Christmastime," Sally told her. "Tell me, have you ever smelled any like it?"

"Never. But you know I haven't seen many houses."

"Forgive me." Sally embraced her swiftly. "How stupid I am! You and Bob have made this room look delicious. When we bring in the red roses tonight—"

"Your trunk hasn't come yet, Mary," Tracy announced from the door. "I looked around again this last trip. Nell's doing pretty well, isn't she, for a girl who has an emergency wedding?"

With his arms full of packages, he disappeared upstairs.

Bob cavorted in from the kitchen, munching one doughnut and waving another which he presented to Mary.

"I'm off for the station. Take your last look at this house, partner. You won't know it for the same place when Aunt Barby's inside it."

"What did he mean?" Mary asked Sally.

"Wait and see. I didn't know Bob felt that way, though. This house never feels the same without Mother."

"Everybody sit down," commanded Molly, "and pretend we have oceans of time. I'm sure it will give Mother and Nell a nice leisurely feeling to see us with nothing to do."

"I get your idea." Midget sank into a chair and assumed a bored expression. "Really," she drawled, "how does one ever manage to kill time on the day before Christmas with a wedding in the house?"

The honk of a motorcar banished the restfulness of the scene. Mary, lingering behind the rush, saw them fly down the path and swallow the newcomers from her sight. She did not "belong" in that gay, welcoming rout. She wished she did. The wishing startled her into consciousness of a strange, stabbing loneliness.

The next minute she heard Sally's voice. "She calls herself Mary, Mother, and we do too. Oh, here she is!"

Mary turned, quietly at ease, perfectly mannered, to meet her hostess. She did not know, afterward, what words she spoke. A face looked into hers, a face like Molly's, older but more beautiful, Madonnalike in its grave loveliness. The great dark eyes smiled at her. As she looked into them, it seemed to Mary Strong that she was looking into fathomless love. She lost her head a little, lost her heart completely.

"Mary is a beautiful name," said the tender lips, giving voice to the sweetest music Mary thought she had ever heard. "I am sorry I was not here to greet you, Mary, when you came. We have wanted you for so long, dear, and now we welcome you with bustle and turmoil."

"I like the turmoil," Mary managed to say.

"You must let us make up for it later," said the lovely voice. "Nell, you and Mary have not had a chance to speak to each other yet. How beautiful this room is!"

"Me and Mary did it, Aunt Barby!" grinned Bob. "Going to be married in here, Nell? You'd better."

"I'll see, Bob," the pretty bride to be threw over her shoulder. "It is sweet of you to come and work for my wedding just like the others," she said to Mary, with a radiant look.

The girl answered in a smiling dream. In a dream she moved about, talked, ate lunch, helped open the bride's presents. Outwardly she conducted herself much like the self-assured young person that she was. Inwardly she burned with a passion to be near Sally's mother, to watch her smile, to see her eyes, to hear her voice. Everything she had ever known seemed to fall into insignificance beside Sally's mother.

The chorus rose around her.

"What now, Aunt Barby?"

"I've found another freezer, Mother."

"Oh, Aunty, look at this exquisite scarf!"

"Give me your advice for a minute, Mother."

"She says she will be over at four, Aunt Babs."

"There's a woman downstairs wants to know if she can't help, Mum, if it's only to wash dishes, Mum, on account of your having been so good to her and hers, Angel Aunt."

"Muvver, can't I have a piece of cake tonight—two pieces?"

"Aunt Barby, somebody's swallowed every hammer in this house!"

"Did you send all Nell's new clothes on to New York, except the wedding dress and the going-away dress, Mother?"

Since she had come, Mary wondered how for an hour the household had existed without the brown-eyed Madonna-faced woman.

"What did I tell you?" Bob asked. "Nobody sees anything but Aunt Barby when she's around. Your trunk didn't come on their train. Naturally it wouldn't. No harm looking, though."

What did Mary care about trunks? What did she care about anything except the gracious presence on which she was feeding her starved-girl soul? The presence that smiled and answered hard questions readily, adjusted difficulties by a single sentence, and never hurried its quiet speech. In the morning Mary had begun to fathom the meaning of the word "home." Now she knew it from *h* to *e*, knew it intuitively after a single look into the face of a woman who stood, children clinging to her skirts and young people laughing around her, in a friendly, woodsy-smelling house.

"If your trunk doesn't come, but of course, it will," Sally told her, "you can wear something of mine. It wouldn't be as pretty, I'm sure, but I'd love to have you."

Mary squeezed her arm. She was catching family ways. Was this girl who ran gleefully up and down stairs, who cajoled tired little Tom out of an incipient fret, who helped Sally set forth the glittering gifts, who fitted in happily anywhere and everywhere, the same young person who had sat bored and blasé in the parlor car yesterday?

Afterward, Mary realized that if they had not all been so busy, it could not have gone on so long. If the sudden wedding had not absorbed everybody's thought and conversation, if Sally's mother had not been away from home when she came, if the family had not had the habit of pet names, if—there were so many ifs! It was only a question of time anyway.

"Really," Midget remarked, strolling into the room where Sally and Mary were putting in place the last wedding present, "what can you girls find to do? Soon I shall be forced to twiddle my thumbs for lack of an occupation."

"You can always look at presents," said Molly, "and later— oh much later!—you can show Katie how to garnish the ices. Moreover, there is the woodshed."

"The woodshed?" questioned Mary.

That question, innocent as it seemed, was her undoing.

"Come and see," said Sally. "Then I must put Tom to bed. If he doesn't have a good nap, he will be cross tonight."

Mary came. On the threshold of the woodshed she paused, dim memories stirring within her, sedate, sober memories, nevertheless akin to the dancing breath-catching recollections of a girl with a different background.

"Tomorrow is Christmas!" she exclaimed as she saw the shimmering tree. "I had forgotten all about it."

Tracy and Sally laughed at the surprise on their guest's face.

"You funny girl! How could you ever forget Christmas? But I don't believe you ever had a really truly merry Christmas! Did you, Mary?"

"Not what you would probably mean by a merry Christmas, Sally. I didn't know the difference, so it didn't hurt me. You will have to show me the right sort tomorrow."

"It makes me want to cry," Sally told her.

"Hand over that box of stuff on the shelf, will you, Sal?" said her brother.

She handed it and fled to Tom and the wooing of his reluctant nap.

"So this is the first tree you ever helped trim?" Tracy asked, pulling shining things out of a box. "I see that from the way you do other things."

"The first *real* tree. But there have been make-believe trees at school, and in foreign pensions the boarders generally unite for a celebration of some kind."

He threw the girl a curious glance. "So you've been abroad?"

"Oh, yes." Her whole attention was given to the placing of an iridescent bird. "You have the loveliest things for this tree I ever saw."

"It looks well, lighted up. We don't generally dress it out here, and usually we have a bigger tree. When people get away and things quiet down tonight, Father and I will bring it in and fix the lights. Couldn't disappoint the kiddies in the morning."

"Then you always have a tree on Christmas morning?"

"Always—with presents for everybody. We had a great tree the winter I was ten; tip touched the ceiling." Tracy's eye kindled. Mary, listening and watching, made discoveries about Christmas trees. The shapely young spruce before her, taking to itself glittering beauty under their hands, stood forth a symbol of all that she had missed. The winter festival of home—pathetic travesty as celebrated in hotels and pensions—loomed before her for the first time, imminent, wonderful. The day before Christmas! Even the snow she glimpsed through the shed window looked new to her; passing sleigh bells jingled with a fresh joy. A well-defined thrill ran up her spine.

She hurried to her room. There were things in her trunk, if it would only come. Things she could give away on the Christmas tree. Mary's heart longed to pour itself out in giving. If she could only find her check! Not that finding her check would make any difference; at such a little station a trunk could not pass unnoticed, but hunting gave her a sensation of hastening its arrival.

It was really pitiful—the zeal of Mary's search. She emptied her bag inside out. She looked through the bureau drawers. She turned up the edges of the rugs. She peered under the bed. And then, behind the dressing table, she saw it.

"I've found my check, Bob!" she cried, flying down the green-wound staircase.

"Good!" Bob turned back from the front door. "Let's have it, and I'll take a turn by the station on my cake collecting."

She put the pasteboard in his hands, her eyes joyous with hope. Save for the two, the hall was empty.

Bob glanced at the slip.

"Hello! Why look here, you checked it to the wrong place. No wonder you don't get the thing."

"The wrong place? No, I didn't. Let me see."

"I'll telephone," Bob was saying. "I'll telephone right away. We'll have that trunk here tonight if I have to send a man over with a team to get it."

"Why no. This check says Crawford plainly."

"Crawford, yes. That's what I'm telling you. It says Crawford."

"But Crawford is just what it ought to say."

"Just Crawford is what it ought not to say. It ought to say East Crawford, the same as your ticket."

"But my ticket said Crawford."

"Then you didn't get your money's worth. The conductor was napping."

"*I* was napping. But I don't understand. Your aunt's letter was dated Crawford. She had marked Crawford on the timetable. I bought my ticket to the address she gave me."

"My dear girl, pardon me—but you're crazy!"

"I am not crazy. Haven't I bought enough tickets, miles of them, to know where I buy them to?"

"You may have bought your ticket to Crawford. Aunt Barby knows where she lives, though."

"But Mrs. White dated her letter at Crawford. I have it upstairs. I'll get it."

Returning, she put it into his hand triumphantly.

"That's no letter from Aunt Barby!"

"Who is it from then?"

"Alicia Coleman White," he read the name slowly. "Who on earth is Alicia Coleman White?"

"Your aunt." She clutched the stair rail, reading the blankness in his face. "Isn't she Mrs. White?"

"She's Mrs. White, all right. Mrs. Howard White. But her name is Katherine—Oh, I say, what's the matter?"

"And this place is . . ."

"It's East Crawford, of course. What have you been thinking it was?"

Mary Strong sat down heavily on the stairs. Her brain reeled. Memory of that horrid moment at the station assailed her. Recollection of references, names, allusions not understood, flooded her mind in one desperately illuminating second.

"It was the car that did it!" she gasped. "She said the car would meet me."

She clutched at one final straw.

"Would you mind telling me—who you think—I am?"

"Emmeline Rittensanger, Emmeline M., I suppose. You're not German, but your stepfather was, and you took his name. Aren't you? Don't say you aren't!"

"I did!" she cried. "I *did* get off at the wrong station. I don't belong here at all! I don't belong!"

Chapter III

The boy and girl stared into each other's eyes for one astounded minute.

Bob spoke first in a quick undertone, "Somebody's coming. Keep your nerve!" Aloud he said, "Come along into the parlor, Mary. I want to show you something."

He hurried her across the hall.

"Look at those flowers," he ordered swiftly. "Keep your back to the door. If anybody should see your face now, they'd know something was up. We've got to think this thing out."

"It's plain enough," Mary said. "I'm in the wrong house. I'm in the wrong town. I've been around the world twice over, and I don't know enough to get out at the right station in the part of the world I was born in."

"Who are you, anyway?"

"My name is Mary Strong. Two days ago I had an invitation from Mrs. White, an old friend of my mother's who lives in Crawford, to come and spend the holidays. She said there would be plenty of young people. She said the car would meet me. I have never seen Mrs. White. I could not remember all I had heard my mother say of her. I knew there was a niece engaged to be married. When Sally talked about a wedding, I . . . I thought . . ."

"Of course, you did," said Bob. "Ginger, but the thing fitted!"

"I didn't know enough to know I wasn't where I ought to be, even when you said things I didn't understand. Mrs. White was the only person I knew by name in the whole household, and she did not seem to be here when I came."

"That was tough!"

"I didn't mind. I'm used to strangers. But you and Sally did not seem like strangers. From the minute I stepped on this porch everything was different from all I had ever known before. That helped throw me off, I suppose. And in Rome I did as the Romans did."

"That was the way to do. But, I say, what a mix-up!"

"I ought to have noticed that your aunt did not ask after Mother," she mused. "You really were expecting someone?"

"They expected you—Emmeline Rittensanger, I mean—yesterday on the train we missed and looked for her on the next train when they found the connections didn't connect."

"And *I* came!"

"You came."

She wheeled on him. "Tell me about the other girl!"

"None of us have ever seen her, not even Aunt Barby. But Marcia's told us about her ever since we were little shavers."

"Marcia?"

"Uncle's sister's stepdaughter. You—I mean Emmeline what's-her-name, is Marcia's cousin. We thought you were a kind of Miss Tom Thumb. Your father died just before you were born, and your stepfather the winter you were five. Your mother died too—something contagious, I think. Anyway—"

"My father and mother are in Japan this minute!"

"I mean Emmeline's people, Mary. I've got you so tight in my head as 'Marcia's little cousin'. But wait a minute! You weren't her real cousin! There was an in-law somewhere. Never mind. With your parents gone, you were brought up by an old-maid aunt of your mother's. We thought you—I mean Emmeline—had an awful dull time. No fun, no girls and boys, all study and great-aunt."

"Is Emmeline also traveling alone?"

"I don't know."

"She was due here yesterday. Where is she now?"

They looked fearfully into each other's faces.

"We're wasting time!" Mary cried.

"Hold on!" He caught her arm. "We're all in a pickle, I admit. But don't you see we can't blab this out to the whole house? It would simply upset and spoil the wedding."

She stopped short.

"Aunt Barby and Nell would be wild," he told her, "thinking of their missing guest—poor little thing—lost nobody knows where."

"But she must be found, and I . . . I can't stay here after this a minute! I can't!"

"Not to give Nell a decent wedding?"

Mary hesitated. "I'm here under false pretenses. And worse still—if anything *could* be worse!—what do you suppose the other Mrs. White is thinking about me this very minute?"

"Oh my! *She* must be wondering too, what has become of *her* guest! Well, we can at least telephone her! But false pretenses? Nonsense! No pretenses about the work you've done. Look here, Mary! Aunt Barby must not know—*yet*. That's flat. Not till the wedding is over and they're off. Uncle's the one to tell. How's your face? Huh! Go out where the Christmas tree is. Let me see if the coast is clear. You look upset."

"I don't," said Mary. "I won't look it. I mustn't, for everybody's sake."

"That's the talk. I'll go and bring Uncle."

"How red your cheeks are, Mary!" Midget remarked as Mary sauntered through the dining room. "Are you tired?"

"I'm excited," Mary told her. "This is my first wedding."

"Has that boy Bob gone for the cakes yet?" Katie demanded in the kitchen.

"I don't think he has started yet."

Mary felt like a conspirator.

* * * * *

In the woodshed, with the tree glimmering from its twilighted corner, she told her story briefly and simply. Bob had already told his.

Mr. White thanked them both. "You have handled this matter very wisely," he said. "I will telephone Mrs. White at Crawford immediately. But I shall certainly ask her to let us keep you until tomorrow, Mary."

"I want to stay—more than I can tell you, Mr. White!" she told him in a voice that was not very steady. "You don't

know how much I wish it had not been a mistake, my coming here."

"You will do us a great favor by remaining overnight," he replied, "and letting things go on as they have been going through the day. It is putting a hard task on your shoulders, but I earnestly ask you to do it for all our sakes."

She answered him gravely, her tone a promise.

"Thank you! Thank you! I will do it."

"Bully for you!" said Bob.

"You are right, Bob. We owe Mary a great deal. Now I will go and telephone to Crawford from another house and put in motion the machinery for locating that unfortunate child. If no definite word comes, after the wedding I shall go myself in search of her."

Bob's eyes followed his uncle's departing figure. "Now it's up to little Bobby to get those cakes." He swung around to the girl. "Mary," he said, "you're all right. Understand? *All right!*"

Alone, Mary retraced her steps through the house. Gladness sang again in her heart. She had a right to be here until tomorrow. Beyond that she would not think. Now she was needed for a service none but she could render. Sally's father had changed the whole aspect of her remaining. She could do something for Sally's mother—for them all. The success of the wedding—that no exciting interruption should mar its joy and happy memories—depended upon her!

"You have been out to see the tree again," Sally accused her. "Tom's asleep. I thought I'd never get him off. Now come upstairs and see which of my dresses you want to wear."

"Which are you going to wear?"

"I . . . I don't care," said Sally.

She *had* cared until Mary came. Now she cared more for Mary than for wearing her new green dress.

"They are very pretty," said Mary, her quick eye accurately guessing the date when each was made—the white and blue and green.

"Try them on." Sally held up the green gown.

Mary shook her head. "The white first. Have you a red sash, Sally?"

Sally was looking for it when her mother came to the door.

"I wonder, girls, whether you would mind dressing now for the evening. The Teasdales, Sally, have just sent word that they are driving over from Painsville, and they wish to dress here. There is no room I can give them except this one."

"There are four of them!" gasped Sally.

"Use my room too," Mary begged.

She could feel all through her the smile of the dark eyes. "Thank you, Mary. That is very thoughtful. I am sorry your trunk has not come. You are sweet to be so cheerful without it."

"Don't you think Mary ought to wear the green dress, Mother?"

"Mary may wear whatever she chooses, Sally. Are you looking for something?"

"My red sash. Oh, I had forgotten this dreadful spot!"

Mrs. White took in the situation at a glance. "There is a piece of red silk in the white box on the top shelf of my closet, Sally. Is that a motor I hear outside? Thank you both, my girls."

The slender figure sped downstairs as swiftly as one of her own daughters, and the girls flew to their dressing.

"Now there will be a rush," said Sally, "just what Mother tried to avoid. Why couldn't the Teasdales dress at home? It's lucky we'll be out of the way early. Tom and Marian can't be dressed till the last minute. Won't they make a dear ring bearer and flower girl? Molly stands up with Nell, and Bob is

best man. It was to have been a military wedding with lots of gold lace. Don't you love gold lace?"

Mary acknowledged that she did. "Haven't you something to do?" she asked.

"Nothing but cluster about at the ceremony. Nell doesn't want it formal. She says we're all to cluster. Afterward, you and I will serve the fruit punch. There won't be many people. East Crawford isn't very big, you know. Why, you poor dear, you *don't* know. We've kept you too busy to know. Never mind, there are plenty of days coming. We're going to eat in the pantry tonight. Did you ever eat in a pantry?"

"Never."

"It's fun. We'll find two big aprons to cover us up. I'll bet Nell is hoping Grant's train will be on time. Aren't you clever to put on the silk like that? The dress is a perfect fit. Didn't your great-aunt ever let you go to a wedding before?"

"I've never been to a wedding before."

"There's Grant! No, it's Father. Supper now, Molly? We'll be right down."

Half an hour later, into the merry excitement of the big airy pantry, came Grant Franklin—big, straight, handsome, unmistakably the officer in the eyes of one who had seen the officers of many nations.

"Hungry? Of course, I'm hungry!" he declared, but Mary noticed that he did not eat much. He was too busy looking at Nell. Mary thought her well worth looking at. Her cheeks were so pink and her eyes so starry, the waiting look lost in a sweet golden-hearted satisfaction.

The two slipped away soon, and before long Sally's mother sent them all upstairs to dress.

"Nothing doing yet," Bob whispered before he went. "Uncle's scared about the accident that delayed *us*. Afraid *she* may have been on that train."

Mr. White made an opportunity to tell Mary that Mrs. Alicia White had agreed to expect her on the morrow. "She found the situation a little difficult to understand," he reported. "Naturally she had been much worried."

He, too, looked worried as he turned away. But he said with a cheery smile, "We'll straighten out everything with her tomorrow!"

Mary and Sally took off their aprons and went upstairs to help in the hooking up of gowns.

"Isn't everything lovely?" Sally sighed for the fiftieth time. "Not one single hitch. Nothing gone the tiniest bit wrong. I'm so happy, Mary. I'm *so* glad you're here."

"I wouldn't have missed being here for all the world!"

As they reached the upper hall, a door opened, and Mrs. White looked out.

"Will you come into my room a moment, Mary? Sally, I think you will have to answer the doorbell until Lizzie comes."

On the bed lay a mass of red roses. Sally's mother lifted half a dozen glowing buds and blossoms. "I want you to wear some of my roses tonight, Mary," she told the girl. "They match the color of your belt perfectly." She fastened them on Mary's gown. Then she kissed her. "You do not know what a help you have been today, dear."

Mary went out of the room in a dream of happiness. She touched the roses with shy tender fingers. *Her* roses. Something within the girl felt in blossom too, warmed and caressed by the light in those great dark eyes. The secret knowledge that she had, put new meaning into Mrs. White's words. Mary felt them as a commission to keep the evening inviolate.

Downstairs a bell rang. She heard Sally opening a door, heard Sally's voice and another's speaking. Suddenly she caught the words.

"I don't understand. This is Mr. Howard White's house,

but she's here. Emmeline Rittensanger is here already."

Mary ran to the staircase. Her slippered feet sped noiselessly down the treads.

In the doorway, facing Sally, stood a girl in traveling coat and hat, a suitcase at her side. She was a little thing, compact and trim, on her face an expression compounded of shyness, obstinacy, and fear.

Behind Mary pounded Bob's pumps.

Chapter IV

Ghe is right, Sally," Mary called softly. "Let her in, and I'll explain."

"Come in! Come right in, please!" Bob lifted the girl's suitcase into the hall. "Awfully glad to see you, Emmeline. You're Marcia's little cousin. We've been expecting you. It's all right, Sal."

Sally looked as though she thought two people, if not more, had gone quite mad.

"Come somewhere out of the hall, and I'll explain," said Mary.

"Uncle's den," Bob suggested. "Nothing there but the punch bowl. Where have you been all this time, Marcia's cousin?"

"There was an accident." The newcomer glanced around her with the air of a frightened rabbit. "Not to our train—to the train before ours. But it held us up. They told us we would get here sooner if we went back and came another way. I telegraphed. We stayed overnight at a hotel."

"You telegraphed?"

"Oh, yes indeed!" The jerky breathless little voice was fervent now.

"We'll get it tomorrow," said Bob.

"Did you not receive it?"

"Not a word. Where did you send it from?"

"From the place where the accident was. I telegraphed I was unhurt."

"Messages piled up," Mary said to Bob. "You know how telegrams do at a time like this."

He nodded.

"I have been all day getting here." Emmeline's lips trembled. "It was not good to go the other way. We had to wait and wait and change and change. And then when I came, she said," looking at Sally, "that I was here already!"

"Bob and Mary," Sally said, "if you are going to explain, I wish you'd do it. My head is spinning."

But Bob wanted to get to the bottom of Emmeline's mystery. "There wasn't anybody to meet you at the station. Ginger! Why, you came on Grant's train! I say, what have you been doing since?"

The newcomer sighed. "There was no carriage, and I had to walk. I walked far, for I took the wrong turn. It was dark. I tried two houses before I reached this one." She turned dubious eyes on Sally.

"You poor dear!" Sally cried. "And we never knew a thing about it! Isn't it dreadful! But what—"

"It's a shame!" Bob growled.

"It was all my fault," said Mary. "You see, I . . . ," she appealed to Emmeline with the prettiest little gesture of confession, "I came yesterday, and they thought I was you, for they'd never seen me before. In the dark I got off at the wrong station and supposed I was in the right place, for I didn't know the people I was going to see, either. It was only this afternoon that Bob and I discovered . . ."

She stopped. Unbelief looked out of the eyes that fronted hers.

121

"And ever since," Bob said cheerfully, "Uncle has been trying to locate you. He has telegraphed and telephoned all over New England, I guess."

But now Sally had recovered her breath. "You don't mean—you can't mean—Mary, if you're not Marcia's little cousin—"

"*There's* Marcia's little cousin." Bob indicated the stranger.

"Then what—who—is Mary?"

Bob undertook to tell her that also.

Mary was talking to Emmeline Rittensanger. "You don't understand, do you? And I can't blame you. I didn't understand it myself when *I* came. For I had never been in this part of the country before. The chauffeur met me at the station and said, 'This way, Miss,' and the automobile brought me here, and I had been invited by a 'Mrs. White' too. They just welcomed me as if they had known me always. Mrs. White was away when I arrived, and the whole household was busy with Christmas and the wedding this evening. So until Bob saw my trunk check with Crawford written on it I never dreamed that—" Swiftly Mary's explanation flowed on. The round, childlike eyes of the newcomer regarded her with unflinching directness. There was obstinacy in the blue gaze, and obtuseness. "Don't you begin to understand?" begged Mary.

"No," said the soft little voice. "I do not understand how any one could get off at the wrong station. Why didn't you ask the conductor what station it was? And then at the house here—No, I do not understand any of it."

Sally wheeled from Bob's story. "Oh, Mary, *Mary!* I can't begin to tell you how splendid you are! You've saved our day for us, that's what you've done. And Emmeline—oh, I'm *so* glad you're here at last! Come right upstairs. Forgive the way I met you at the door. We'll make up for it, never fear. I am so sorry you've had such a time getting here and that you arrive just when every one of us is in such a rush to be ready for the wedding. Mother will give you a welcome that will smooth out everything, but oh dear! I *can't* call her just now, when the wedding is—mercy!—right upon us! Have her trunk brought up from the station, Bob—quick. Somebody will be downstairs soon. Midget must have gone in by now to help Nell dress. We'll put Emmeline in Midget's room."

"Let me take her up," Mary suggested. "I'll help her dress."

"Oh, will you? You're a dear, Mary. I *must* see to so many things, and there isn't a minute left." The two girls vanished.

Sally lingered to whisper excitedly to her brother, "We can't stir them all up now, Bob. Why, I . . . I feel as though I'd been sitting on a volcano and it had erupted."

"But Aunt Barby'll see her, Sal!"

"Of course, she'll see her. But if she doesn't come downstairs until after the guests begin to come, Mother will think she belongs with one of them, and the guests will think she belongs in the house. Everybody will be perfectly sweet to her. Wait and see!"

"She thinks we're a private lunatic asylum," whispered Bob as he hurried off.

"You must be very tired," Mary said kindly when they reached Midget's room.

"I *am* tired." The blue eyes looked longingly at the bed.

"Lie down for ten minutes. You will have time enough. I'll be back in a moment with a tray of lunch."

With food and rest, even the scantiest rest, the small face took on happier curves. The eyes grew less obstinate. Mary made herself as charming as she knew how, and Mary knew very well how to be charming. As soon as Emmeline's trunk appeared, she helped to open it.

"It is scarcely wrinkled at all," she said, lifting out the visitor's party gown. "You packed it beautifully."

"My great-aunt packed it," said Emmeline. "She made it too."

"She made it out of your eyes," smiled Mary. "It's a lovely color."

Emmeline fingered the dress as though she loved it. As Mary helped her to adjust it, she glanced at the watch on the dressing table. "We must be quick. I see it is time to go down."

There was suppressed excitement in her voice. She could not remember when she had felt as interested in anything as she did in this wedding of a girl whom she had never seen before today.

"You look very sweet," she told Emmeline.

A quaint little blue figure slipped down the back stairs beside Mary.

"We will slide in among people as though we had been here all the time. The bride will be coming down in a few minutes. There's Mrs. White—in black with the red roses—over there beyond all those people. Did you ever in your life see anybody so beautiful?"

"No," said Emmeline, "I never did."

She said it honestly, a little breathlessly. Her eyes lingered, fascinated.

At that moment she and Mary began to like each other.

"She is a wonderful woman." A little old lady with snapping black eyes and silver curls smiled at them. "I remember when Howard White brought her here as a bride."

"She must have been exquisite," said Mary, "but somehow I have an idea I like better to look at her now than I would have even then."

"Living," said the little old lady. "It's living that's put in her face what you mean, child. But when she was young, with that grace and sweetness, you couldn't match her in the five states. Nieces of hers, aren't you?"

"No," said Mary. "We're no real relation. But she is as sweet to the girls that aren't as to the girls that are."

"And always was. Well, my dears, you're not the first to love her."

"Who was that?" Emmeline whispered as the little old lady turned to the people on her other hand. "And what did she mean by the five states?"

"New England, I suppose. I don't know who she was."

"But you talked with her."

"Oh yes!"

Mary ran her arm gently through Emmeline's. "Come and let's talk to other people."

Sally's father spoke to them warmly. "Tomorrow we shall begin to prove to you how glad we are to see you!" he told Emmeline. "Tonight you won't believe us, I'm afraid."

Sally's mother passed among her guests. Emmeline's gaze followed her in worshipful mystification.

"She doesn't know yet that you are you," Mary whispered. "They will tell her after the wedding."

"Come and help us cluster around Nell," said Sally. "She doesn't want a stiff, pokey wedding. Of course, you're coming, Mary. I've nearly burst trying not to tell people about Emmeline—you're such an adventure, you two! I thought I'd dreamed it till I saw you together."

"Glad to see you, Emmeline," Jim said. "Uncle told me. Your coming is a wedding present worth having." He turned to Mary. "You're a brick!"

Music stole out of the nook under the stairs. The minister took his place; Grant Franklin and Bob joined him. Slowly, a bit one-sidedly from the necessity of always putting the same

foot foremost, a small white-suited figure descended the stairs. In his right hand, he carefully carried a ring in a small flower-trimmed basket. Behind him trailed the deep rose of Molly's gown, and behind Molly a white fairy, equipped with Marian's serious, little-girl dignity, scattered glowing petals in the path of the slender white bride.

Mary's heart skipped a beat. Nell, in the filmy cloud of her veil, was beautiful. Mary had seen pictures of brides in newspapers; she had not dreamed they ever looked like this! There was something in her throat. Had she read that people cried at weddings? How foolish to cry when you were happy! She dared not look at Sally. Sally was gripping her hand too tight to make it safe to look at her. She watched Nell and Grant, the young gravity of Bob's countenance, the shining look on the face of Sally's mother as she stood beside her husband. *Christmas Eve!* thought Mary. *A new home was being struck off from an old home on Christmas Eve.*

And then, before she realized it, the thing was done. The two facing the minister turned about; people pressed up to them, smiling. Laughter and joy were around her, but over Mary there began to rise, imperceptibly at first, a tide of loneliness. When the little waves curled about her feet, she hardly noticed them. She had done her part—nothing had marred the wedding, and she was glad. When those waves rose to her knees, she waded on valiantly, her head high. What if she were a Cinderella for whom the clock was set? The waves closed around her heart, and behold, her heart was no longer the floating India rubber thing she had known so long. It had developed roots that clung and held.

Nobody dreamed that unhappy thoughts were assailing the girl in the white gown with the red roses at her belt. The heads of the roses drooped a bit by now.

"What pretty manners she has!" the guests said.

"She's all right!" said the boys.

"Mary is perfectly charming," Molly told Midget. "I don't see how she ever learned such ease and poise, shut up all her life with only a great-aunt for company. She's prettier than I thought she was too."

"She looks waked up," said Midget. "She has been growing to look more waked up all day."

* * * * *

The bride's cake had been cut and eaten; the ices and the punch had disappeared; the harp had fallen silent; most of the guests had gone. Bob walked over to his sister where she sat between her aunt and Grant Franklin on the great davenport in the living room. Bob detected interrogation in the look Aunt Barby bent on Emmeline Rittensanger.

"Wonders who she came with and why she doesn't go. Diplomacy, thy name is Robert!"

"Doing pretty well to have only one pair of duplicates among your presents," he said to his sister.

"I haven't any duplicates, Bob. Not yet. We've been lucky about that, Grant."

Bob grinned. "Where are your eyes, I'd like to know?"

"Now I wonder what you're driving at," said Nell.

"Bob has something up his sleeve," remarked his new brother-in-law.

Bob appealed to his uncle. "The duplicates are in this very room, and they can't see them!"

"I'll bet *you* don't, Aunt Barby!"

"In this room?" Nell questioned. "Presents to me?"

"Presents to you."

"But all the presents are upstairs, Bob," Molly demurred.

"We wouldn't have had as fine a wedding here, if it hadn't

been for those duplicates I'm talking of, and they're in this room fast enough. How about it, Trace?"

"I guess the wedding would have been pretty slim without either of 'em on hand."

"You know, Tracy!" Midget accused him.

"Father and Jim know too," put in Molly. "And Sally."

"Mary?"

"Yes, I think I do; indeed, I am quite sure I do." Mary's cheeks were pink.

"Don't you know, Aunt Barby?" Bob pleaded. "Give a guess. You're warm."

Mary held out her hand to Emmeline Rittensanger. "*We* are the duplicates Bob means, Mrs. White." She smiled bravely. "They are going to exchange me tomorrow."

"I don't believe in exchanging things," Sally cried, "no matter how many duplicates you have! Can't we manage to keep her, Mother?"

"That's the talk!" said Bob.

"Hear! Hear!" echoed Mr. White.

"Ditto," said Tracy and Jim.

Mrs. White drew the two girls down on either side of her. "What are you all talking about? Of course, we shall keep Mary, now that we have her at last."

"I wish you could," Mary said. "But perhaps you won't want to when you know that I'm not really a duplicate at all. I'm a missent package." It was very hard to go on, but she went on steadily. "I came to the town and the house that I wasn't addressed to. You had never heard of me, Mrs. White. It has all been a mistake, a lovely mistake for me. *She* is Emmeline Rittensanger."

It took a long time to make everybody understand, and even then the quaint little figure with the gentian blue eyes felt still a little bewildered and not at all certain what might happen next in this strange house.

Through it all Aunt Barby kept fast hold of both girls' hands. Once she released her right hand to pass her arm protectingly around Emmeline's shoulders. "How thankful I am that you are safely here!" said the low sweet voice. Once she kissed Mary. "And I have to thank you for my peace of mind today. I should have been almost sick with fear."

Before every point had been cleared up quite to the family's satisfaction, Nell and Grant had to go away. "You have been the best wedding present of all!" said Nell and held Mary close in a warm, furry embrace. "I like duplicates."

* * * * *

When they all came back from the station, Jim and Tracy brought in the Christmas tree.

"We'll be in no hurry to go over to Crawford tomorrow," said Jim as they set it up.

"Don't even *think* about tomorrow," Sally begged. "Let's sit up as long as we can, to keep it from coming."

"I know a fellow in Crawford," said Bob. "You'll see me over there."

"Will you come sometime and visit us, Mary?"

"Will I? Oh, Mrs. White!"

Mary dropped to a footstool beside the slender, black-gowned figure, and a hand drew the girl's head to the silken knee. Molly's fingers began to stray over the piano keys. The others gathered about her. Sally slipped Emmeline's arm through hers and moved toward them.

"You don't know what a revelation this house has been to me," Mary was saying. "I was born on ship. I have been traveling ever since I was born. I have seen a good many things in different parts of the world. I had begun to think there wasn't

much that I had not seen. But I had never seen—a home!"

The gentle hand smoothed the girl's hair tenderly. "That is where journeys end at last—at home."

"Mine hasn't any home to end in."

"Perhaps your father and mother are tired of traveling too."

"They can't stop," Mary said. "Father has done it too long. He took a villa just out of Florence last winter. He meant to live there. No, he can't stop, literally. We live in trunks, not houses."

"In a few short hours you have made a home for yourself here, for you have won all our hearts. You must always feel that our home is yours. And some day, dear, you will have a home of your own."

Mary lifted her head. Her eyes glowed with the light of newborn faraway expectation. "Some day I will!" Her tone was a resolution. "May I come here sometimes—did you mean it?—and learn how to make my home?"

"*May* you? Why, we shall never let you escape from us now. You *belong* to us, dear."

And Sally's mother kissed her.

Mary dropped her head again upon the silken knees.

At the piano they were singing carols.

God bless the master of this house,
Likewise the mistress too,
And all the little children
That round the table strew.

"I think," said Mary softly, "that I got off at the right station, after all."